An Uncertain Void

Ooda had always been different from everyone in her tribe, she noticed when she was quite young, capable of picking up net weaving, and repair, watching her father, by the river estuary. She had tried to introduce an “el” sound to their local dialect, during her teens, in an attempt to add a sense of present dayness to just the activity of “hunt”, but people just thought she had too many fermented berries and had a lazy mouth.

In their small tribe, not too long after a great ice sheet had nearly taken the planet, Ooda was a much more capable member of the tribe. She was key on a hunt, and had developed a hole surrounded by water trapped in stone, which was colder than the outside. Salting and curing, and storing foods so their tribe were never hungry. Some of the skills she displayed were attributed to the forest itself, a daughter of their local god; Nature, protecting them on account of their worship. Never attributed to Ooda herself; she found herself lamenting it too often, but never told anyone.

“Lost?” The noises made by Rai, intelligible to Ooda, were not likely to be understood by a modern English or indeed Spanish, or ancient Mayan speaker. “Forbidden tree, not far. Don’t Listen, if no mouth!” the warning given by Fera, uttered and mimed by Ooda, trying to remain quiet, in case they could add to their list of fertile territories.

It was late in the day, the sun sliced through the trees, the angle giving the light a green tinge through the thickness of the forest. Ooda had pushed them deeper than they would usually go, she wasn’t sure why, but knew there was something better going deeper. It was only the two of them now, most had gone home, happy with the day’s successes, and getting low on water.

“Rai?” Ooda muttered softly, having been distracted by the low lights across the forest. They never were never in the forest this deep with this kind of light in the day. “Where are you?”. At some point in her perimeter sweep of this evening verdancy, he must have wandered off? The thought held in her mind optimistically. They were never here this late. “Rai?!”

Scrunching the note from the door into her pocket, John heaved open the surprisingly well hinged, oak door. Out through the stale smell of the doormat in the smaller porch, onto the wider decked porch, down the steps, and towards the haphazardly parked cars outside. “Wait a minute John,” Arachni blurted while trying to catch the now swingin closed door, “Where are you going? Where are we going?”. John paused for a second, before turning on her heel, “You’re right,” she said, striding back towards the door, “Provisions.” her glasses masking her eyes as she smiled sweetly, moving past Arachni, who had now been pressed into the door to make way for John's return.

Arachni followed John’s biker boots which were making a dull thudding along the wooden floor with each purposeful stride, through the house to the kitchen, where the tone switched with the transition to tiles.

As Arachni rounded the corner, from the hall into the kitchen, they were met with the sight of John using her forearm to clear shelves of the fridge. Scooping into the strangely elasticating inside pocket of her jacket, meats and vegetables, condiments, and platters of h'orderves; presumably from a previous club party. There didn't seem to be any sound though of their fate inside the pocket, no shatter as glass beer bottles toppled in with equally vulnerable glass condiment jars. ” Provisions.” John announced on Arachni’s arrival, with the prideful lip curls of a soldier preparing their kit for battle; pleased with their perceived readiness. “What’s with your coat John? And, honestly, can you stop for just a second and explain to me. What are we doing?” Arachni’s voice raised with frustration. “There was blood in that room, and do you know that one of those cars out front belongs to a police officer?!” Arachni’s voice rising further with each dangling and dangerous thread of their situation. “He was a good person, what if it’s his?!” John by this point had moved to the cupboards and was trying but failing, to tactfully continue placing individual cans into her pocket, maintaining the head position for eye contact, behind the shaded protection of her glasses.”These people are murderers..and,” Arachni boiled over to a vented simmer,” you’re prepping dinner?!”.

“Is this your first time?” John had taken all the food she needed from the cupboards, and now hung her thumbs inside the edges of those same pockets. Arachni’s thoughts wandered for a moment as she scanned John’s posture. What would happen if she put her thumb all the way in the pocket? Would she lose it? Would it stretch?

“My first time?” Arachni replied with spines, “My first time with murder happening, everywhere, apparently, and no police to speak of?...Yeah!”. “Well, this is not my first time seeing this.”

John's calm reply delivered like a salve to the prickles, “You have been cast, by whatever it is that weaves these things. You do not choose it, it didn’t even choose you, it just is. And you know what?” John paused and lent forward on the kitchen island in the middle, dropping her tone to an ominous whisper of secret truths to be revealed. “It’s far better .....to just always have some food on you.” She lent back against the counter behind her, adding “I even get to give some away to people who need it.” She folded her arms defiantly, as though closing the argument.

“That is not the problem here John!” Arachni let loose after letting John’s complete missing of the point get to them.”Aren’t you afraid of the consequences of this? Of police? Prison? What if we die?”. “Well, of course we’re going to die,” said John with a matter of factness that irked Arachni, “Everyone dies.”. “Don’t be facetious, this is real, there’s blood! In the next room John?” Arachni’s vocal expressions had moved from irate to incredulous, a little shaken with relief from the release. “Like I said, this isn’t my first time.” John’s reply with a slight smile in the corner of her mouth. “You can choose to run away from things or towards things, but there’s going to be things, sometimes like this, sometimes better. But sure as anything, you’ll die in the end. Gotta at least enjoy yourself, or not fight the tide, or fight it all you want. We are in this story, this series of events, and you just…. don't want to be hungry on top…..or thirsty." She chuckled and fished a beer bottle from her pocket, removing the cap with leverage from a knife on the drying rack of the sink beside her. "Are you high?" Arachni blurted. "Not yet," said John, "Look," she brought her voice to a less flippant register. "I don't want to say what will happen, because I don't know, but I've not run into police around these guys. I don't know, I guess they're in it, or they can use what this guy already did on those people in the diner. I have no clue. I told you, I will follow the rumble.You got to find your own way to go with it you know?". "You saw what happened in the diner?" Arachni's question held out as a dual enquiry on how long John had been watching them.

The room was the temperature it was supposed to be, a soft mattress, on fresh sheets, the smell of the detergent, like a kind of safety; waking up the Detective, the crook of his elbow aching slightly, the cold steel of an ankle cuff confirming to him the situation. At the end of the bed, merging into individual focus, a willowy woman, of indeterminate age, and the second figure; a shock of yellow, atop a purple face.

“Lilian?” the detective groaned out the greeting half question to the slowly materialising, attractively familiar, willowy woman standing at the foot of his bed. He had woken up with more painful hangovers, but this was the most coagulated his thoughts had felt in a good few years. How long had it been since the night at the club? It seemed like the room had a bright window, but he couldn’t make out anything through it. His mind drifted to the pain in his elbow pit and wondered whether this was more than a standard IV, he would have to pull it out when they weren’t looking. “You said, you’dn’t take part in this stuff?” his best attempt at a comedy-casual question, formed with a mouth that wasn’t as complicit as he’d have liked, considering the company.

Peril tried to shuffle his body up onto the pillows behind him, hoping to mask his arm movements and continued in spite of his impedance “You…, this is all boys club sbloney, you said, you said medicine. Are you?”. The detective fell deeper into the pillows behind, unable to support his head on his neck, or self on his elbows. That same willowy. and familiar outline drew herself closer to the detective. “But, I am in medicine Folsy. How do you think you made it here in one piece?” her voice gentle as Folsom had ever remembered it, asked rhetorically. “You are in the way of something important we are building.

Like you always were I guess. Jessop and I, we were looking at the compound you took in the trees. It's… unbelievable the things we can do with this knowledge. Oh Folsy, if we could get everyone to understand, the good it does so you can connect your mind." Her voice mirrored the kinetic type of excitement the detective recalled in Jessop from that day in the great tree. "People would live stronger, longer lives, fewer health problems even at age, and then…. But you already know all this don't you? " her voice trailed off as she adjusted the covers up on the bed, shifting a small piece of hair from his slowly close fluttering eyes." I can keep you safe here. It was meant to happen like this, don't you see?" her final rhetoric echoed into the detective's thoughts, as he slipped back into welcoming blackness.

Agent Staff had been a part of the Earth's Suppression Outreach Team, or ESOT, sometimes OTES for obscurity reasons, for over 8 years, and was as dedicated an agent as any other. It was a prestigious organisation, or held itself as one, with many rebrandings over the years to reach the perfect in ambiguous titles for a branch of planetary governance. Their task, to keep all of the humans focused on planet Earth, its future, and misdirected from access to information that the species was not ready for, as a whole; or at least, this was the doctrine the Agent subscribed to. It would be like handing machine guns, with armour piercing bullet technologies, to mediaeval knights; a quote from a superior which Staff had felt resonated perfectly with her mistrust in the population's ability to do, what she believed, were, the right things.

Taking long strides for her height and in sensibly rugged combat boots, which did not match the rest of her well pressed suit, Agent Staff strode across the wide country road between the tree banks, searching the road both ways for traffic, but none was in earshot. Her destination, on a small roadside, encircled with more tall redwood trees, the OTES issued SUV. There were no identifiers of its authority fleet status, no lights on top, crests, coats of arms, or badges, just the metallic green paint and the fact she didn't have to pay for the fuel; which was a plus.

As she moved across the empty roadside to the car, her hands shook in her pockets, she clutched the phone in the right outside jacket pocket as though it might break out and rampage across a nation. Agent Staff had been on the trail of one of the biggest corruptions in her particular branch of governing in living memory, she had a witness willing to testify waiting in the car, and had just taken video of an execution. Not in the dark and ominous way that it sounded, but an unfolding of a horrific chain of events that, in its sinister way, she needed. She was finally ready to take this up the chain, to wipe the smirks from the faces of her colleagues who told her not to worry about this organisation. “They’ve been around forever Paula,” Agent Staff recalled the condescension of her area leader, when she had said she was going to the lodge to investigate the links to the groups leader. “It's just coincidence, trust me, we wasted a lot of resources on them before. It was before your time but trust me. Many better representatives have been caught up, trying to be the police. We are not, I repeat, not the police. We can detain, in serious circumstances, but come on, take it to the police if you are worried about missing persons. As far as I can see there are no credible reports of them doing anything to commit to a mass reveal. Our job, spin, obfuscate, and if it's bad, wipe em. And you seem hellbent on getting to being a toast burning, wannabe detective officer again. The Guidance *are* with us.”. Well, Agent Paula was feeling both vindicated, and shaken to her core, as though her investigation was coming to a close, but she had only scratched the surface it seemed, she had never felt more in danger. As her fingers reached under the door handle, she cast her eyes around the emptiness of the car parking area, before looking through the car window and noticed something was wrong. Where was the witness?

The sun had long since left the sky when Agent Paula Staff and her star testimony had crunched into the layby in the now empty SUV. “Chip, I’m going to need you to stay in the vehicle for me, while I scout ahead on this. According to my map, the lodge should be just through here.” her gaze locked to the tree line opposite,”... and you said the whole back window is glass?” She turned her head back toward Chip but didn’t need a reply, but was awarded a nod.”That should help things.” The agent ran through her plan not really to Chip, but to herself, as she usually did in her head before any major meeting, although this was not like her usual investigations, she couldn’t risk memories being wiped here. What are the key points, how do I deliver them; she was preparing, this was the one.

“You know this could get quite serious, if they succeed, they might take away my role in the administration,” Eck had been pining self importantly to Klo on the porch for at least long enough for it to become tiresome, since John and Arachni had disappeared into the house for provisions.”Not just for me though, if they have records of it ALL, I mean some of it is very familiar to the eternal myth.” Eck’s half sentences half questions to the wind, were getting frantic. “What are you talking about Eck, sometimes, sometimes, I think you should just take your own advice, and not interfere.” Klo tried to stem the flow of introspective concern spouting from Eck.”You didn’t assume to be in your current position, but, you are there, as sure as you will be somewhere else.”. “Don’t patronise me Klo, I am a Galactic ambassador. I’m just concerned, what if our myths and their myths combine? Or. Human beings are so few. Who would have thought they could get themselves together like this. They always seemed so isolated.”

Ooda had been searching for Rai for too long; the thought in her mind, as she saw the shadows of the trees starting to swaddle the leaves and branches into a violet moss around her. Finding a way back would be treacherous. “Rai,” Ooda softly muttered across the dark, her eyes expertly strafing the undergrowth for protruding limbs, or the ovaled eyes of four legged predators. It was the lack of sound entirely that put Ooda into a sense of unrest, why wouldn’t he answer? The forest was never quiet, not at this time of day?

Then, almost as if exactly timed, Ooda recognised a gentle murmuring coming from the otherside of a particularly thick tree trunk and lower canopy. She brushed it aside and emerged almost as if through a waterfall of foliage into an open hoof shape. Or it felt like it. It stretched around and out of Ooda's peripheral vision, in the middle, stumble-running horizontally across her sightline, disappearing on the right and reappearing on the left, the muttering Rai, smiling a helpless, exhausted smile but not stopping. "Rai, what do?". Rai disappeared into a point and reappeared again, in the distance, from the other end, still half running, a clutch of purple berries in his left hand, leaking into his fingers. "Stay!" Ooda moved across the cooling evening, the sun bending a thin odd-pinked orange arch with edges of the navy rising night spreading to the edges of the treelines, like the inside of the rolled leafs smoked on special occasions, but without the materials inside. The hollowed inside of a spear, but more beautiful. She grabbed Rai by the top of his forearm as he approached her intercepting perpendicular track, Ooda squatted down into the immaculate grass, bringing him to a stop with her motion. Rai smiled a purple tinged grimace gratefully, before toppling onto his side. "What?" Ooda asked again at Rai, who was gulping air like water for thirst. Rai muttered meekly, "No talk, No Mouth".

As the sun traced down the sky, in a park, behind a hut, that seemed a long time ago now, Chip Winner's eyes fluttered into focus on the outline of a suited woman, with silver aviators; the trees and blurred concussion had robbed his vision of any further study."You're awake," her captioning helping Chip into the situation, "I notice your coat, and of course," she paused raising her head toward the hut, "the location we are, are you a member?". Chip recalled his mandatory induction, and the protocol in case the society was about to be revealed."I'm just a citizen lost in the woods. I must have fallen over." Chip knew he'd made a fine job of that nonchalant response as he concussidedly half smiled at the now tilting shadow of Agent Staff. "Yes," she cut through this blatant lie, "My name is Agent Staff, or Paula, I understand you know this man?" she placed between her body and Chip's face, her phone screen, brightness to full; the all too unique side profile of Jessop was clear as day to Chip.

As John strode out of the kitchen and back into the familiar boot thuds on the wooden floor, she continued, "You said you wanted to know where we go next, well, help us out, I have to go, if you have to go too, then something should just… you know?". She flicked her wrists and shoulders up to the sky with the flourish of *I-don't-know-what-to-tell-you*, "Does anything stick out to you here, are you feeling drawn in any direction?". "What do you mean drawn in a direction?" Arachni blurted in what was becoming a more familiar tone when dealing with

John. “I don’t have a rumble John, I’m not a game controller, I don’t.” they trailed off to a more even temper. “This is something I am getting used to, and your lack of specificity is starting to get to me.” . “Have you even tried?” John asked, shaking her head before the answer could be made. Arachni cast a gaze around the walls and the facets on the circular vaulted ceiling of the entrance foyer. At first, running across paintings, parchments behind glass, small tools from early civilizations on display, each with some spider like design. Some of them in glass cabinets, but by the door, there, an ornate bowl; as a result of distance, it appeared like wide-set wicker, but closer to, as Arachni approached, was a wood carved, webbed bowl, complete with its own three dimensional long limbed spiders, separating keys. A set that flashed into Arachni’s mind from under the hand of a spider candied sleeve, in a diner a few events ago now, suddenly almost pulled their hand out toward it. Arachni held the keys out to John as if they were the answer to her question in its action, but clarified. “We’re going to need a car.”. John smiled, “You sound like a wally, throw them here let’s go.”. “What?, I was drawn to them.” Arachni protested feeling robbed of what felt like the first time they had some feeling of control on events and threw them to John. “Well, yes you were drawn to them, but that doesn’t mean you get it yet.” John pulled the front door to the lodge and activated the unlocking clunk flash of Perils car while doing so.

“They’re quite dramatic these ones,” Eck commented as Klo appeared next to him on the parcel rack of Peril’s automobile. “What do you mean dramatic?” asked Klo, knowing there was no choice in the matter but to indulge him. “Well,” returned Eck, triumphant in his bluster, “They spend such a long time bickering and chattering about things, and not a lot actually doing things. I said to John, one of the reasons she is a familiar of mine is her ability to just do. You know, less of this, I will, I shall, should we shouldn’t we, which can hold people to apathy.”. “You enjoy conversation in this realm though don't you?” Klo was still not accustomed to the leisurely pace at which most humans interacted, and considered whether Eck was trying to train her in endurance.”Oh very much so yes, they do offer the ability to spread a thought over a little longer a space than otherwise might have been given to it. I wonder to myself often on days like this, on the warmth of this ground, in the relative safety of our existence, now, at least as we see it, bound in this set of events, whether we are wrong to see it as beneath us. Perhaps, maybe we can lose ourselves in infinity, in the ever lost feeling of anything, and can’t see the now, but the now is everything for these things, and somehow. Should we not tell them, I worry that by asking it might stir up their desire to know more, and then it might lead them to it anyway." "Are you talking about these prison records?" Klo asked impatiently, "Do they even realise how close this could all get to being a big mess? Sometimes I watch it and wonder? But it never hit us Klo, this could change everything for us, this could break things I don't even understand. And I have a very long existence area, deep, wide, and varied." He puffed himself up into the sun beams streaking the parcel shelf of the warm dust moted car. "When do we need to worry?" asked Klo, feeling a little more concerned than before. Eck deflated slightly, and muttered "Now.".

"Look, all you have to do is be ready," John continued her sermon to Arachni as they both dropped themselves to the butt into the leather upholstered seats of Detective Perils voiture. "I don't mean the sky is falling yet you see Klo, I am just telling you, you need to be ready," Eck tried to assuage the concern he could feel emanating from Klo. It seemed to shake his physicality like the car engine as it turned over, bone rattling the car into ignition. "So all we need are snacks then, and a car?" Arachni sarcastically asked the already non sarcastically, affirmatively nodding John. "It is the most you can prepare yourself in my experience," John reaffirmed her point, pulling the car out from the long gravel and bark crushed driveway away from the lodge and out onto the main road. "So how are we supposed to prepare for this, whilst not involving ourselves?" Klo asked Eck as the sun trilled its branch shaded fingers across the parcel shelf. "Well, we need to get all of the information first of course," Eck tried to bluff, "Once we know, then we will know what we have to do.". "I thought you said you knew what you were doing though?" Arachni queried John's unwaveringly confident forward stare into the road beyond. "Well, once things are more clear, I can see a way through, but at the moment, we just need to make sure there is enough food, for when we don't know what to do?" John reached into a side pocket, fishing out a carton of grapefruit juice, pouring it deftly, with only a minor glance for accuracy, into a plastic tub, taped onto the parcel rack. "You see," Eck said, moving to the fresh poured grapefruit juice, "John is prepared, and we are fine. Sometimes," he gulped and continued with satisfaction, "I think we have to trust these humans have this covered.". Klo couldn't pull the kind of expression Arachni might have in this situation, but the feeling inside was equivalent to incredulous, existence questioning, wonder. As though the leader of a nation had told you war was to be determined on the outcome of a game of rock, paper, scissors, between two chickens.

“Let’s try this again,” sighed Agent Staff, as any bemused enforcement officer might, as she helped Chip to his feet. He was swaying slightly with an arm and hand buttress supporting the head. “I know you are with the Guidance, I saw you enter an interdimensional storage area, without any concern for passers-bys, who were uninformed. You could have caused an incident.” She lowered her glasses and could see Chip's glazed focus following very little of what was being said. “ I need to speak to this man” She brandished the phone screen at his face for a second time.”You know him as a, Brother Jessop” Agent Staff maintained a wary eye on Chip, who still would not have made a great escape on the legs beneath him at that time, while she scooped up some keys and other detritus that had somehow left Chips person, she knew how they had left, but would not be pursuing anything just yet. ”I think you should come with me,” Agent Staff hooked under Chip's arm and helped him to wander back out to parks waning light.

“I just joined ‘cos the weather 6 guy joined one,” Chip half slurred, ”I never thought it’d go like this you know.” After a few minutes of Agent Staff's no nonsense striding through the nightfall cooling park, Chip seemed to believe he had been caught by the police, and was now in a full confession mode, making sure he distanced himself as much as possible from any potential for recrimination in the future. Of course, due to his current cognitive function, it sounded more like the apologetic football player, caught taking an illegal stimulant, and now has to make a public apology, but they actually were a good person, and it disappointed their mum, which made her cry, and makes them cry on top because they just wanted to make her proud. " I haven't even been in long, and I can help you, they're having a meeting, it's something big, and they're all going to be there. I can show you. I don't know if I can be." Chip hoped that his performance was working, he needed to figure out a way to get a message to Jessop that OTES were coming.

Chip purposefully made a meal of his injuries the entire way back to the car, trying to keep this authority, which one was this, he wasn't sure but he needed to get to a phone."Am I in custard?" Chip asked faux-sorrowfully, "No, we just need to understand a few things that have been happening here. What happened to the third man that entered with you, for instance?" the Agent paused glancing across Chips frosted dull eyes, "It seems as though you need medical attention, so we will get you feeling steady first, then deal with what you have been doing." The Agent quickened her pace and the pair arrived at the OTES SUV only too soon for Chip, who was only now beginning to realise how this concussion was muddling his mind. Was this the police? “Am I the rest?” Chip asked again, trying to embellish his condition but genuinely struggling with mouth movement beyond a slur.”Almost there Mr Winner, you mentioned a lodge we were going to?” Agent Staff thought she might try her luck, although not strictly ethical, this was a lead too good to pass, something inside her told her, even though she was not usually one to thumb the scales; it had to happen this way. “Oh yes, it doesn’t really have an address you know. I have, there's a link on my, I’ll show you, do you have a map in your phone?”.

As Chip softly closed the car door, still feeling somewhat muddy in the mind from earlier, he wondered if this betrayal of Agent Staff's kind nature might be a problem in the future. It didn’t matter, this was a chance to be something, to seize a chance to something. He knew he was more than just an attractive weatherman, he was integral, a main thread, in how the world discovered. Everything. He had guided the Agent to the layby perfectly, he knew the area well as a back entrance to the lodge for extra curricular activities with some of the more attractive members. A little further up the road there was a simple wooden gate entrance to the reflection garden, from there he could get to the house.

It must have been over 20 minutes since Agent Staff had left Chip thought to himself alone; lent against the cold car side panel, he knew he could make it to the other side of the road without an issue. Chip stoop-ran across the road, just out of precaution, scrambling in smart shoes up the mudded embankment and down into the woodland area behind the lodge's maintained garden, but still on the land. As he caught himself on the trunk of a tree for balance, he could make out, facedown in the mud, and in that familiar blazer, a few trees in the distance, ahead in a clearing, Candi from security detail. Chip thought about stopping, but wasn't sure if he had the time to waste. He managed to send a quick text to Jessop from the Agent's phone while they were in the park, pretending to struggle with using the mapp app to find the destination. A feat he was feeling much more proud of considering his current rising nausea. Chip strode along the more beaten mudded path in the wood to the rear door of the reflection Garden, and could soon make out from the vantage point, the grand dining hall window, hidden under the sill beneath was a crouched Arachni, and equally foetal positioned John from the security email. Chip slowly backed out of the reflecting garden, trying carefully, but failing utterly, not to trip the security light.

Only a few hundred metres away from Chip, poised behind a moss dampened, and fallen log, Agent Staff had her phone trained on the Panoramic back window of the lodge, like a wooden bezeled television. This is unbelievable she thought, steadying her tremor from the adrenaline, this is not just a disappearance, a suicide, some other non culpable act. She saw, she had recorded, in, was it bits, or electrical charge, there was evidence, clear, people died. There was an officer, she recognised him from before, how is this all coming together. And why do these two keep showing up everywhere? Particularly John, she was meant to be a rumour. As her mind klaxoned with anxiety bells, and fear, neurologically flushed with chemicals, there was a small flash of a security light and the click of a garden gate. Did they know she was here? Staff was not going to wait around and risk not being vindicated, or worse executed like she had just witnessed. She pocketed the phone tremulously, keeping her hand pressed to it so it wouldn't, couldn’t, escape the coat pocket, as she stalked her way on a retreat arc from the scene of the crime.

Lilian Pad, was at maximum stride as she lent back in her chair, everything was coming together, something not even Jessop could foresee, so lost in his vision to supplement himself to blindness. She allowed her gaze to drift out of the floor to ceiling arched window, the sun overcast by cloud on an otherwise clear sky, far to the harbour city in the distance, it's glistening waters beyond, and closer, to a steep and crisp pine gradient, out again to a more deciduous forest below, between her, and the traffic, the noise, and the people. When Jessop came to her 18 months ago with a vision, she had already been on a journey of her own. even further than edges of the water as it somehow didn't quite touch the sky, but lapped its edges.

"Professor Grehnikin, and Dr Pad, what is your intention here?" the customers officer at border control asked, seeming not to check their faces from behind darkened glasses, a necessity in the bright white room. "We are here on a mission of discovery," Lil was almost too excited, and drew honest scrutiny from the officer who would normally not have paid much attention to two, well, he might call them "science types". This kind of nervous uneasiness on the feet of this woman as she seemed to be rolling back and forth on her feet, was what he would expect from someone with something to hide, but these cases were chrome, locked and sealed, with tapes of varying complexity. Just to open it could take an afternoon of international calls, conversations with Jenny the interpreter, and things had been awkward there for too long, a whole afternoon with her, no, in the end, they seemed to check out. "We have papers from Biotyme if its assistive in any way? We have a schedule to keep, we should have been there last week." Lilian excitedly, effervesced, she was hoping the enthusiasm might detract from any notion from this border officer to check the contents of their baggage. Not that there was anything to hide, but just the time to go through it all, for the third time on this transit. "The weather in this region though, so unpredictable at times." Lilian continued to witter to the guard, she had entered countries as a scientist thousands of times in her career, with samples and without, with equipment, and without, but this had been the most fraught with checks, every border seeming to have an issue with her passing. Perhaps it was the presence of Grehnikin. She wondered if this was a sign of things to come, or if this was just the culmination of probabilities from journeys unchecked. "I've never had problems before this," Lillian hissed out of the corner of her mouth to Grehnikin, "It must be you, what have you been up to, are we going to have to explain all this? Again?". "I thought you liked talking about our work?" Professor Grehnikin, casual and calm as ever, turning with a quarter smile of smoulder to Lilian.

instantly diffusing her anxiety countdown. “ We have to the hotel here anyway, it’s too late to start out yet. What’s wrong with another keynote address, and then maybe something relaxed, in the bar,” He cast his eyes and head around dramatically continuing, “ I hope they have.” Grehnikin always had that flippant attitude to any situation, as though danger was just an appointment to be kept endured and moved past, an amuse bouche for a cocktail. It was what had drawn Lilian too close in the past, but that charm would be essential in finding some of these villages, which were too far off of any track, to have ever feared a beating. They grabbed the chromed handles to the heavy corrugated, wheeled cases, and shepherded them through the security boundaries, and following Grehnikin’s keen identification, across the tiled concourse, to the ubiquitous airport bar. Even without the seminar on their gear, both travellers were ready for anaesthetic.

Lilian lent on her palm, allowing her cheek to smoosh up into her temple area. They spent months trekking the forest, speaking with locals, learning new dialects not even recorded, trading information for help, for supplies.They had claimed to be on a fact finder for Biotyme, a company that Lilian had been a senior project lead in new biochemical process designs for.

They were going to source some of the original berries, berries Lilian remembered from University days, with her favourite professor Grehnikin, berries that could only be sourced, according to the professor, in a remote part of the Amazonian rainforest. The plan for Biotyme, was to cross engineer it, with a more hardy plant to produce the berries in a less challenging environment to cultivate. Some simple gene splicing, or maybe husbandry, and it would be resolved, the potential for profit was limitless, and these could genuinely help people, Lilian had assured the head of the grant committee of it.

The truth though, Lilian knew the future, it was not going to be a supplement, the grand awakening that Jessop wanted, with the intrinsic deaths that accompany a mass april foolsing like that. When you pull the rug out, someone is bound to bump their heads on the edge of the fireplace and die. Somehow though Jessop believes this number will be low, but imagine the unrest, when they see how stagnant we have been. No, the way of taking the lead over people was never going to be the way, not in Lilians heart, she just wasn't paying attention to the humans to begin with. And while she wasn’t paying attention, she picked up a few friends from other planets, who had their own stories to distract from the world at large. It was in this assimilation of information on a grand scale that sewed the seeds of the only future Lilian could believe in. An ancient power, bound, the great unravelling. No more would humans be bound to Zelon futures, but free, to construct their own interweavings.

As she felt her mind truly dissolving through the window into the outside, the warmth of the now emerged sunshine on her face welcoming her to answers of the future, a glass timbre knock announced the presence of Jessop outside her door. “We have another guest to visit.” his statement, more command than request, but Lil was happy to oblige, she had some questions of her own.

Fumbling the cool, painted metal door bolt closed on the garden, Chip took a moment for his eyes to adjust again to the darkness. If John was here,he thought to himself, he needed protection, this wasn’t a straightforward warning of police, this could be a rescue mission, or even a stand alone story, of taking the lead. Being a leader, and being strong. Chip wasn’t sure, but as his eyes scanned the darkness for foot placements, his thoughts swept his mind for ideas, and quickly settled, that Candi, ex-champion fighter Candi, would be able to shoulder the difficult parts, while he would still be there, in the end, a name in the books. He picked his way back through the increasingly less manicured woodland, towards the spot he had seen her last, planking a mud puddle.

As Chip approached the area he remembered her being in, he found a sight he had not thought of as being so beautiful before. Crouched against a tree, checking with her finger and phone camera, with torch full beam for missing teeth; of which there were none in this digit wrangled smile, the mud streaked face, of Candi. “Candi,” Chips whisper-shouted through the trees, incase they weren’t alone, jerked attention, and an index finger, from Candi’s mouth. “It’s Chip, from the founders fondue, do, I was, I wasn’t very fond of ew, cheese, it was ….a joke, you were…. Are you ok?” Chips garbled anecdotal identification was enough for Candi to relax her shoulders, she recalled his clumsy conversationalism, she also was confident that she did not have to seek any dental assistance. “What are you doing here? John is on site,” Candi quickly slipped into a security and debrief mindset. ” I tried to intervene,” she touched briefly the red-purpling side of her face that had received the impact, “Guess I got lucky, she moved my mouth guard though, so I wouldn’t choke, that’s…., the notes mentioned security risk.” Candi lost her focus a little, possibly from the injury, but possibly on the thought that maybe John wasn’t what she had been led to believe. “I am fine,” she continued recalling Chip’s, until then, unanswered query, “I didn’t know you were in the lodge, are you ok?". "I wasn't, truth be told Candi, I was caught by some OTES agency trying to silence us, and, I mean I let Jessop know by text, but," Chip turned his head gravely to the halo of light in the direction of the lodge "Candi," he hardened his tone, "We need to get in there," he motioned with clasped finger guns, "You mentioned John was on site. I thought that she was taken care of in that diner, I mean I sent two good guys." he allowed himself to trail off, in plastic memorial, "We have to save everything, this could be, this could be, the world, at stake Candi?" The last few words held with pause in hope of inducing a feeling of magnitude. She looked at him incredulously, he seemed oblivious to her recuperation from the last encounter with John. "I think I am going to wait here then," Candi responded flatly, "If there are police or authorities, I am not getting myself arrested, or worse losing teeth over this. Come on Chip, it's a club for the sake of breakfast." Chip looked blankly for second at her; puzzled with the word choice, "Candi, this isn't just a club, I know you have not been privy to some of the deeper truths we can offer here, but people could be hurt," he paused again hoping to summon some sense of occasion from its space,"You, you are their protection, I know this doesn't happen often, but when it does. Don't you, owe it, to the honour of the position, to rise up and…". "Why are you not doing it then?" Candi cut across quickly, well aware of this tactic, “If it is so noble, why aren’t you running in to save the day.”. “Candi, beautiful, MMA Champion, Candi, athletic, skilled in this kind of scenario Candi. Or just me, I mean I lift, we all know I can move if I have to, I just, some people are just....” Chip produced from his pocket an elegant fountain pen, which elicited Candi to mimic his action, producing her own pencil from inside her blazer. “Do you even understand what it is that you are Candi? This is more than just a symbol, you are capable of drawing and erasing, changing the very lines of our fate. And anyway aren’t you supposed to love this fighting stuff. It's not just to give you that phenomenal figure is it?” Chip smoulder-smiled the last of his barrage of hopefully subtle enough, ego boosting, commentary to initiate the response he needed from Candi. I mean, no one was expecting him to go in by himself, and risk losing the knowledge of the, the books and all of the, he was very important to the organisation..... as an arbiter, advertisement for member benefits. Death would not be a benefit even he could sell.

A long way away from the tribulations of Chip and his task to be an expert convincer, Agent Sleep had been trying to figure a way out. Only two days ago, or at least he hoped that long ago, he had been outside of a diner with his partner at OTES Paula. He was just trying to humour her tin foil ramblings, but was sure of their tin nature no longer. “Seriously Sleepy, this is is a genuine exposure plot that could actually succeed, we need to do something about it.” Sleep recalled Staff tirading for the third time in their monthly briefings about these leads. He was just indulging a theory, he never genuinely thought things could end up, wherever this was. The room he had awoken in only a day ago was the kind that you might expect from a high end, self catering, holiday flat, rental. The bedding and fixtures were just high enough quality to give the illusion of quality that was profitable from visitors only selecting based on image quality in an app. He didn’t feel like he was being held in a prison, but certainly this would not be a homely feel to a room either, this wasn’t the bedroom of a house. The door had security netted glass, and was locked from the outside.

He and Agent Staff, or at he had, been what expected a routine clean up on an exposure event. Apparently some diners had witnessed a breakdown of a disciple of the eternal and unfathomable. These things happen. It was not uncommon in their line of work, many disclosure attempts involved people who had come to understand, or at least to perceive, from their perspective at best, how much of a puppet of fate they were; they felt compelled to forever cut, any strings, to anyone or any act, not realising the act itself, of cutting the strings, was the act of the string twichers, the endless undulation of time, rippling decision and action of millions. There is no escape it just is. This incident though, it seemed, or at least from the information they had managed to obtain, that nonone actually saw it anyway. There had been footage on a phone, which was mostly contained, spun into obscurity, and welded tin helmets, on any sites it existed on. This was important. Agent Sleep was a firm believer that people, the population, had not yet learned to share well enough, to share the knowledge that they had not yet been given the opportunity to grasp, not in any structured educationally standardised way.The knowledge that could corrupt as well as it could encourage, that could be used for the quick ends of profit, for the self, rather than benefit of all.

Agent Staff had peeled off to follow an alternative looking suspect with a rucksack, Paula was curious why there seemed to already be a detective on the case to begin with, only to discover that this person was not associated with OTES at all. Staff had always been headstrong in following her instincts and being honest. Agent Sleep, in a similarly instinctual sense, had not been able to follow his normal morning ablutions schedule, and was now very much out of sync, and uncomfortable. He took the opportunity to take this time alone to have a comfort break, in the diner's pleasantly hygienic facilities perhaps he could get his head round where this might be going. It couldn't be as serious as Staff was making out, but still, it was a peculiar event, surrounded in peculiarity.

He couldn't have taken more than five minutes to complete his leavings, but thereafter his timeline becomes muddled, until the waking in this room. He wasn't sure if he ever left the commode itself, but definitely had distinct memories of sunshine in his eyes; the swing-click of the door closing behind him. Had he been struck on the head? He allowed his right hand to fingertip-graze over the contours of his skull, but finding no lumps, or unrecogised one, contusions, or crusted scabs. He couldn't place how he had got here, was Agent Staff in trouble? Why could he not recall any details either. He knew he had to focus on resolving his own situation first before resorting to any rescue attempts on as yet, unconfirmed kidnapees. Where was this? He strode halfway to the window, only to identify in closer focus that it was not the outside, the beautiful video image of an outside, water and mountains, presumably somewhere, maybe somewhere here? But not there, not that space, where there was no window. As the realisation set in, almost in serendipitous sympathy, the door lock and handle clicked open, revealing with its soft swing, the purple faced man from the other day, and a willowy looking scientist that Agent Sleep was not familiar with, before clicking closed.

"If you're so prepared, why didn't you think to go before we left in the car then John?" Arachni scolded John, as this was the only refutable evidence of a lack of preparedness she had displayed since their meeting. "You couldn't have included toilet's in your provisions?". John side eyed Arachni as they pulled in to a layby, knowing she was just following the rumble, that ultimately, she had to follow the machinations of the story, there was no choice, it was when it was time. As the tyres popped and scrunched in declaration of their arrival, John's focus was pulled to the unexpected presence of another vehicle, strangely early, definitely not a hunter, considering the lack of bumper stickers, dents, scuffs, or gun rack. As the car crawled to a stop, Arachni had given in to the situation, accepting the sounding off as venting stress akin to an inmate at their prison guard. Ultimately, they were there for the duration, better learn to adapt. John quickly unbuckled, swept out of the car; closing the door with equal efficiency, and was soon scrambled over the embankment which marked the edge of the car area of the layby, into the undergrowth, to find a secluded spot. As the door closed, Arachni realised they had been awake too long, and asleep too little. Perhaps a moment or two, just to look at the eyelids.

Since hearing the sound of an engine rumbling up the road, Agent Staff had chosen to flatten herself out on the rear seat of the SUV. Her mind buffeted by the crashing of thoughts against her skull, the murder she witnessed, had evidence of, the loss of her star witness; was he nearby, was this car just returning, double checking, had she made a mistake returning. As she strained her back to look through a small gap between the pillar of the car door and one of the rear headrests, she wondered, if sometimes, she was a little too reckless. As the thought crossed her mind, a shape seemed to whip out of the car and over into the woods, the coat though, recognisable even in a glimpse. Paula knew, at that moment, as a spark flew between her belly button and coccyx, this wasn't bad luck, this was manifest prophecy.

She rearranged her skeleton carefully trying to shift weight without causing the car to rock, even with SUV suspension, she couldn't risk it. There was a second silhouette in the car, but it had seemed at rest, it could be another victim of this cult, and they could be burying bodies. Agent Staff continued her contortion between the front two seats, and over the handbrake, to grab the phone, and OTES issue self protection tazer. She placed the phone on record, and slipped it into her breast pocket, allowing the phone to rest on her homemade silicone buffer block, so she knew she could get the perfect held shot, like a real body camera, which her department were yet to receive.

Oblivious to the anxiety turmoil, turning a furrough inside the mind of Agent Staff; inside Peril's torpid leather-seated sedan, Arachni was at the base of a severe stamina drop, a trough of emotion, action, and information; leading them flickering their lids into a fretted snooze.

Arachni had been standing under the softly chattering trees for an hour, or a minute, or they were not too sure, the sky though, twisting a copera dance battle between daytime and night time, was not a usual sky. As Arachni's head swept left, the expected tree line and forest were already disintegrating, as they focused into the more acquainted contours of the banqueting hall from the lodge. Just as the sky though, the wood, so fanatically addourning and fashioning the fixtures and furnitures of the room, was more orange, or it might have been red tinged, the sound of dull footsteps on the wood, a figure that could not be seen. Or at least not yet. “Arachni?” a familiar Peril toned voice drifted in with the vision of the man himself, but again, orange tinged, like a white shirt after a mismanaged bolognaise. Not orange, red, “Arachni, it’s been too long,” the outstretched arms of Detective Peril like the encroaching bite from a B movie zombie. “Stop,” Arachni found herself shouting. Even though they knew this couldn’t be real, Arachni found themself backing toward the door to the kitchen, pressing it open and into the chromed, and tiled quiet beyond. Only, there was a familiar clear wall of window, that wasn’t where it should have been, as if the had been stretched on one end, beyond its thick clarity, the forest seemed, the branches appeared to be floating in arm thick as the water. A surreal pale grey bird, with eyes too large for a normal bird, butterflew its wings, swimming up into the fading sunshine. Arachni approached to lay a hand on the fragile solidarity of the glass. Its texture, not cold, but on touching, the fingers and palms of Arachnis hands began to sink into the cooling glass, leaving them to tumble, again into the darkness of the Ocean beyond the window.

After what seemed like too long, “You are a fish,” the Ocean’s comforting surf tone interjected abruptly, “No,” Arachni corrected, trying desperately to find up, but realising quickly there was no up to find, accepting to feel thoroughly disembodied in this floating. Where are the trees? “I am not a fish, I am a human.” Arachni gave in to the curiosity to speak, to what could well be only another part of themself, their mind, talking to themself, about everything that wasn’t themselves, in a way neither party seemed complicit in conjugating . “No, there are many fish, fish only know the water, only flick their tails and make their waves close by.”. “Well what about shoals of fish then?” Arachni queried, “If a large group of fish, all made their tails flick as you say, at the same time, in a concerted effort, couldn’t they do more?.”. “Oh yes, many fish are strong, but they only know the ocean. Even big fish, lots of them, they don’t want to work together enough and make waves together.” Ocean continued nonsensically, “You be a whale, know the air, see land, make a big wave.”. “I don’t understand what you are talking about, how can I be a fish, and a whale?” Arachni, somewhat fed up with the Ocean’s inscrutable nonsense, asked with fire. “It is simple, make your brain, the biggest fish in the ocean, we all share, by not being a fish.” the Ocean chuckled to itself. “The thing about whales though Arachni,” it continued to giggle “they need to breathe….”. Arachni gasped awake, almost inhaling her own tongue in the process, sweating slightly, the leathered chair sticking to exposed skin, in the layby, under the trees.

Four seconds in, Agent Staff’s mind keeping count as she expanded her thorax, four seconds out, she repeated the process in reverse allowing the weight of her ribcage and collar bone, coupled with the squatted position, four seconds in, to allow the air to be pushed back out again for four seconds. It’s unlikely a murderer would drive around with a body propped up on a passenger seat, but the tinting effect of spying through two car windows made it difficult to find details of life. Paula continued her breathing, keeping the sound as low as possible as she crept round a depression in the muddied embankment, separating the woodland from the rest area. It wasn’t as if anyone would, or even could hear the breathing, just Paula’s own self consciousness of the act. Placing her hand to the surprisingly dry ground for support and balance, after travelling a what felt like halfway around the perimeter embankment, she peeked over the top, checking her bearing with the new car, the passenger still with a head cocked back, seemed to be casting a short condensation on the window, which was heartening. A slow creeping relief began to spread in Paula’s mind, she straightened up her walk slightly, moving with less stealth, more caution, around the mudded mound; hopefully she could catch whomever it was driving on their return from the undergrowth.

Agent Staff continued her advance, slightly on the blades of her sensible hiking shoes, until, after a few premature peeps over the bluff, she could see herself in parallel with the car. Crouching slightly lower onto her knee for support, she reaffirmed the positions of the phone and the taser, pulled in her belly button to the base of her spine, coiled to strike. As she raised up, as a righteous valkyrie into battle, pushing hard off her right foot, in a purposeful blitz, up and over the raised embankment, her left foot caught in a root, she mistook for an attempt at a leg grab, causing a half turn, and self powerbomb, off the mud, on to the less forgiving loose gravel, and stone space edgings. As her chin was whipped, from her chest to the sky, on the impact of her shoulders with the floor, a long coat, and green mirrored sunglasses, began to crest over the view that was blurring out.

Some miles away from the powerbomb in the parking lot, Chip had managed to charm, or perhaps erode with sycophancy,

Candi into joining him. “I just…” the sound of one large, and one normal sized engine cars, could be heard rumbling to life and then out of earshot in the distance, “.... maybe we should see what’s going on.” Candi concluded, hoping the danger was over, but knowing for some reason, they couldn’t have entered the building before then anyway. It was that tickling in the marrow of her bones, a discomfort in remaining stationary, she got when something was about to happen. It had only happened a few times before joining the Guidance, but since then, she knew it was not to be ignored, but unsure why. Through the undergrowth the pair walked in a pseudo military recon filing, to the wooden gate. Two heavy executive sedan door clunks could be heard through the wooden slats as Candi held the handle of the gate; gently releasing the latch with her thumb and sliding in and around the door to the reflection garden, being careful to stay wide of the security light’s detection. Planning tristes for some of the more married members had provided the opportunity to gain such a discrete entrance route. Maintaining a low posture, she turned, tilted her head under her raising armpit, and whispered back through the gap, “Follow my footsteps exactly, we don’t want to draw attention to ourselves.”. She motioned, as a lead might to a unit, with two fingers, around the edges of the hedges, to the corner of the stairs.”It seems we might be alone, but trust me, we still need to be careful." Candi warned him as they drew to a stop at the stone edge of a water feature. Peering through the cool air coming off the water slowly rippling from the gently trickling water of the figure above, "I think we should move in through the lower conservatory, the door has been on the latch since last month……" Candi realised the company she was in, "Don't report me for telling you that. It's for the kitchen, there's always smokers in the kitchen."

"You just, shared your status with someone else. I thought that was forbidden?" Candi wanted to get a better understanding of Chip before entering, if he broke those rules, could he be counted on. "Oh, come on Candi, almost noone follows that rule, people can't help but compare themselves. I mean, I have quite a status, but I have always been jealous of your type.". "My type?" Candi replied with an amount of scepticism poorly hidden, "Were you not paying attention? Didn't you read the literature? Pencils, particularly with erasers Candi, are symbols of noble destiny. You don't get chronicling privileges such as myself, where I provide the ornate fill, but instead you. You're. There are those. Who are meant to guide through change. Who's destiny is partially crystalized, like an icebreaker boat's bough, in more ways than just the ice crystals themselves, you are capable of carving new paths through what felt like a solid immovable. Of course, not invulnerable, potential land mass beneath the ice, or even stubborn ice, an eraser to the lines. Nonetheless though. Candi. You should have pride, can you not feel, our presence, here, together, is one of great importance?". The bombastic deluge had elicited a reaction of quietened, confused frustration from Candi, who had now stopped her stooping path along the lower planters of the conservatory, and was staring with one finger to her lips, the other hand holding an imaginary sandwich plate to the ceiling.

"Why talk with no mouth?" Ooda's scornfully pitched question to the still panting Rai was met with an outstretched palm of oozing purple berries, which Rai promptly wiped with disgust into the grass. "Berry bring voice, then run, but Rai not run OOda. Rai stop. Rai stop." He repeated the phrase as he continued to heave breath back into his lungs. Ooda, scooped a small amount of the berries from the ground, placing some in a leaf into her bag, with the remaining residue on her fingers, she sniffed gingerly, hoping some smell might indicate something about the mystery berry."I wouldn't eat that if you're anything like this one," a haughty voice inside Ooda's mind, she spun around, slowly 720'd, wiping the remaining residue back onto the now twice stained with purple grass. "Smart decision," the same voice, goading another twist around from Ooda, "Who?", she said to the sky, the trees, the bush she had come through. "I apologise for your friend there, it seems I might have met the wrong one. My mistake. I am Earth ambassador, Eck.".Ooda reached down for Rai, urging him to come with her, off over to where they came, away from the mouthless voices. "Oh I have a mouth, well of sorts" came the voice without a body again, Ooda hurried her pace toward the tree line. "Ooda?".

Her name, how did the voice know her name? She stopped and pushed Rai forwards through the bush in front of him, turning back and dropping low, she reasoned it must be very loud or very small to be that loud so close. "Yes,very good." the voice of Eck came through like a sarcastic conscience. "Come now, I wouldn't be here if you weren't ready to get this, I mean…. look at your friend. If you decide to follow him back that is. Too much, some of the other local, non guide types. He was open to all kinds of, not everyone is going to be nice about it you see. I am tasked to be a guide for your species to understand more about the universe. You are, apparently, the first of yours to be curious enough. But yourself, you seem ready?" These words, that Ooda had never heard before, but instantly felt an understanding for, the first real conversation she…. her mind felt as though it was crackling like embers of dry firewood. “Where?” Ooda laid flat to the grass, feeling somehow heartened by this friendly voice, which seemed to meet her own feelings of haughtiness over others.

“Just a little beyond where your eyes are moving now.” the unsettling thought that it could see through her eyes, instantly answered, “Only when it makes sense to. You see we or at least I, am, to myself, a student of your species, and its time. There is a lot that we don’t really need to get into. It's important to note, we do not want to interfere.” Ooda did not get a new word, for the first time in her life.”Or, hmm, not yet. To stop you being your sunny human selves or your own destiny. We just show the ones who need to, or find their way here, or, well there are a few ways, but we don’t need to get into that now. Do you have anything to offer for your membership to the network, a memory or a song or something.” Ooda reached into her bag and pulled a medium sized grapefruit she had picked as a treat the following morning from the small net hanging on her side. She broke the top quartile off, pressing her thumb in to make a bowl of juice and set it beside the now apparent small spider moving through the blades of grass toward her.

Sleep was rarely afraid, but there was something about this willowy woman's softness that set the alarms in the hallways of his mind, filled with his years of work accessing liars, on full klaxon. “Well Agent Sleep, do you mind if I call you Tom?” “Well, it seems permissions aren’t something you go for, so why even ask?” he wanted a reaction from these two, mostly her though, Sleep needed to understand what this was about, he couldn’t wait for a rescue on this. OTES as an organisation, was really an organisation that, well at his level, he might not be noticed for a day, or a fortnight, and he was not going to wait around for it, like an idiot, and if these two were it, or had a key, or a phone. “Let’s not be rude to each other, you are a guest.” her voice again too pleasant for his liking,”Guests are invited,” he cut across defiantly. “Well maybe some people in this life we just aren’t meant to get along with, but in the end it benefits us both, if you go along here. I am sure my colleague explained to you, we don’t want anything from you, we just. Your partner, is just particularly good at evading us, and we actually want to speak to her as much as she seems to want to speak to us. We just need to steer things a little, and have a few cards in our favor.”. “So I am an involuntary guest card in this weird kidnap hospital of yours? You realise that Staff has been onto you guys for ages.” Tom raged definitely, “If you think it's not gonna be, they’ll be coming round the mountain, or whatever, lake view this is before you will see it coming." Sleep flourished in full bluster. "Oh we will see it coming Tom, it was all seen coming, and you would know to go along, if you could see the way that we are able to." She clasped his hands in hers, the weight of the much larger bones obvious to both, maintaining his gaze, fully aware of his impotent rage. His eyes darted from his defiant stare down, and away, she knew she had won, if not his trust, then his submission to the situation. A realisation that she had the control here. "Now, you have been asked to maintain a dream journal for us during your stay, can you show us how that has been going?".

In a similarly decorated room, a few minutes prior, not too far from Agent Sleep, Detective Peril's plan was starting to come together. He had been careful to maintain as much eye contact with Lilian as he could while he had trapped the IV tube leading into his arm between two fingers. It had taken every ounce of his strength to keep it held long enough for his two former college colleagues to leave so he could, with a grimace, remove the needle entirely and make a more permanent pinch in the tube so it wouldn't be obvious it had been removed. He knew, as he felt his mind spinning, that it could be a while before his full functions and faculties would be returned.

Detective Peril was sure, as he lay, still with remnant heart palpitations and sweat accumulating between his body creases, that he wouldn't be disturbed. It had been a whole ten or maybe fifteen minutes since, what he assumed must have been an orderly, had passed to check on his status. The footsteps along what sounded to the close eyed, but awake, barely, Peril, were on a linoleum floor or some other plastic. It sounded more like a hospital, but there did not seem to be any patient noises from other rooms, if there even were other rooms. Maybe it was longer, Peril wasn't sure, but he knew, this was not the time to check an imaginary stopwatch. With great effort and purpose of thought, he clutched the crook of his elbow crease, whipped his legs across the bed, and down onto the floor under his own weight. As he brought himself up from the right angle, the effects of his stay became more apparent, his shoulders felt like they were being pulled backwards and to the floor. This was clearly going to require a lot more resistance on his part than he was used to in terms of intoxication. Maybe not even an intoxication, his mind was not fuzzy as it had been, however long ago it had been, Lilian playing with his hair, what was this drawing his knees into the floor? He felt his body weight shift back beyond his shoulders and hips, almost twerking backwards to hold himself together.

The first thing here was to see if they had been foolish enough to put his belongings in the same room as him.

As he stood there, his elbow crook still feeling the tendering effects of a needle, but under the warm comfort of his palm, Peril took a moment to gain his bearings. His slightly tunnelled vision moved from corners, along walls, jerking between targets, providing very little information in the detective's addled state, other than a block-form floor map to the door, and locations of a blurred brown shape, which could be small cupboard, or another door, and bed-side table with a drawer. The drawer was Peril’s first stop for investigations, it was the closest, and his mind he knew, the one he could access without a potential for misbalance. Haphazardly, he fumbled a grip, and yanked the drawer open, seeing his clothes, and surprisingly, the detective's shield, neatly stacked; emanating the soft smell of floral detergent. He tried to glance at the door for a moment to check for spectators, whipping his face without much control toward the door glass, and then back to the drawer, feeling as though his brain had bumped his skull in the process. Well, he thought to himself, if we’re going to have any chance getting out of here, I need to get at least some of this on.

It took some time, skill, balance, and the special ingredient; years of drinking more than he could handle, for Peril to have such a proclivity for moving under this current sense of encumbered movement. Sliding his legs into his trousers, while perched back on the edge of the bed, he managed to catch his heel several times in each leg, as he dragged them up his thighs. He decided against buttons on the shirt, having wasted at least a minute to no avail on the fastener of his trousers, instead deciding the belt would be enough to hold them up. There were no footwear options, beside the hospital slides slid neatly just under the end of the bed. After attempting to walk in them however; Peril knew he could move neither quietly nor comfortably in them, and they were abandoned.

Peril took his first lumbered steps across the room to the tall brown box that was coming into focus. From the bed, he had assumed it was a cupboard of sorts, but as he almost fell forwards on to it, placing his hands in its middle for stability, it was confirmed. Another quick check of the reinforced glass window in the door, and Peril had opened the doors to garmentless hangers, and a piece of paper scrunched in the corner. Returning the paper to its full size, provided only one clue as to where he was; a familiar watermark on the paper.

The light of the day began to take hold, heating the air in the layby under the trees, Agent Staff's eyes flickered back into life with its intrusive brightness; her surroundings at a different angle to what she had recalled. Before the world had slipped from beneath her and delivered a power bomb that even the most experienced wrestler would struggle to shake off. She scanned the scene, she could see her own car, blocked slightly by two figures, one she recognised as the, could-have-been-corpse, but actually was a sleeping passenger riding shotgun. The car she had been approaching was now, as she peered over her shoulder, the backrest for her recovery, and two heel marks led through the gravel from her tumble to her current slump.

As she sat there on the uncomfortable floor, shifting her hips for a less jagged position, but finding none, the mirrored green glasses she recalled prior to her cut-to-black was tilting her head, the OTES issue taser hanging from her left hand. She was leaning in and whispering to the second figure, a beige leather jacketed individual, was this another member of the guidance Staff found herself wondering? It was not possible, the mirrored glasses woman was known to OTES, or at least to Agent Staff, as, if not an enemy of the Guidance, certainly a persona non grata. Guidance sources had issued security warnings not to approach her. So why were they with a member? Was it just a coincidence they were wearing beige, or a disguise? Agent Staff knew that if these two were really out to hurt her, they would have left her in the layby, maybe alive, maybe not, but this, this was concern being displayed. They might still kidnap her, or worse, she wasn't sure, but if she played this right, she knew, somehow deep in her gut, she could feel she wasn't in the danger it might have looked like from the outside. She could turn this back on them, she could use this as an opportunity.

Prior to the Agent's awakening, John had made sure to check her pockets, collecting up the taser from the unconscious pile of crumpled person, and taking a brief perusal of her pockets. The wallet contained very little in money, which John did not need anyway, but sometimes it helped to keep a stash, just in case. The wallet did yield a more important piece of information though, the laminated, officially stamped, badge of a bureaucrat. John had always tried to remain outside of the purview of OTES, ESOT, or Earth's Suppression Outreach Team. They were mostly concerned with disclosure, and John had never had an opinion or thought on it, she just followed her instinct. She had never really dealt with anything quite this wholesome before truth be told, and finding it all just a little bit tiresome to not get to use the full extent of her destined skills. Also, that chick from the woods was hot. She looked up from her searching, as a bleary eyed Arachni emerged from the car, raising two platefuls of what's-going-on-here to the sky. "You can't even go to the toilet without causing injury can you?" the slightly croaked voice of Arachni asked rhetorically. "Help me with her will you?" John hooked an arm under her shoulder and the pair pulled her body across to their car, propping her into a seated position.

John took the assorted belongings of the Agent, and went across to the SUV, "You keep an eye on her ok?" John said over her shoulder, "What do I do if she wakes up?" Arachni asked with trepidation, "I'm not like you John, people don't just, I don't fight people.". "You seemed to do just fine with that Guidance member in the woods, you'll be fine." John's word, sparking yet more curiosity in Arachni. "Wait, you saw what happened in the diner John, and the woods? Have you been following me a long time?
And you didn't step in, why? John do you even care?". She stopped with her hand on the door of SUV, turned, "It's not about caring Arachni, this is going to get very old very fast if you keep asking me why I am doing what I am doing. Why did you pick those keys? Why did we turn left? Why did I have to

pee? Why was she here in the first place?" John had released the door and taken a few steps back toward Arachni, her arms wading through her own questions as she did so. "I don't know, but what I know is they were the ones skulking in the woods with a taser Arachni." she pointed toward the slumped Staff with her chin resting on her chest. "They're from an agency. You asked about police" John tossed the wallet with the badge inside to Arachni and returned to the car door that was ajar, "Why don't you ask her?" John disappeared into the SUV, leaving only her feet sticking out, as she felt inside door pockets, footwells, and glove compartments for anything that might bring the rumble back, and mark the return to their journey, their story, the destiny.

"Who are you?" Arachni, the beige leather jacketed figure, from Staff's perspective, kicked off the interrogation, "and why are you following us?". "I was here first, you followed me." Agent Staff said defiantly, deciding to stay seated so as to appear more vulnerable, and maybe get these two to open up. "Yes, but you were the one skulking the woods with this weren't you?" John chimed in, spinning the taser in her hand. Agent Staff switched her focus to the mirrored green glasses, "What would you have done in my position? I don't know if you realise this, but I am a federal…." Agent Staff was cut off by John chuckling. “Oh come on, you’re not a federal agent like a cop. There are no stickers on the car giving detailed information on the world so many people are not ready to join yet. We weren’t doing anything wrong, why did you need a weapon? Why sneak around?”. Agent Staff felt a little flustered, authority was usually her best bet for advantage in a situation like this, but this green aviator-ed woman was not one to kowtow to it. “OK,” said Arachni changing tack, “You were here first, but what brought you here? Let’s not pretend we don’t all know there is a Guidance lodge through those trees. Are you with them? Are you trying to stop us from getting to them? You know there is an actual police officer who has disappeared?” Agent Staff was used to the disrespect, and honestly agreed that she was no police officer, she considered herself above such a position. More of a politician, or spokesperson for the Earth, not a local enforcer, capturing criminals and the like. She had a higher cause, the safety of the species, the protection of knowledge. She fixed her eyes on the beige jacketed Arachni, wishing she still had her own aviators on to disguise her expression.

Eck had not ventured far on Earth, in spite of his obsession with human culture, his experiences with the current form of the species had been less than what he expected. That being said, he had never eaten something quite as good on Earth as the fruit he now sat in, enjoying its sharp but nourishing juice. “I think this will do nicely,” he paused in his replenishment, “Ooda, would you like to follow me?”. She had been sat cross legged on the floor, admiring the tiny spider, wondering how many other animals might also be able to talk like this. Had she hunted other animals like this? Were their howls and shrieks words, warnings, cries for help? The spider suddenly appeared on Ooda’s shoulder causing her to fall backwards with shock, “Don’t worry Ooda, you know that feeling you have had, as long as you can remember? The one you get trying to explain the world to the others, and the others, even Rai there, look at you, like you should be sent off to the quiet shelter. That dwelling off in the forest, where they put your mother.”. Ooda felt the weight of that pain swell inside her, she had always struggled to explain to people what just came to her without effort. Thoughts that people hadn’t thought, and so couldn’t yet be articulated, or when they were they were dealt with suspicion. The attribution of all of her inventions to the forest itself. “Yes,” she said slowly. “Well,” came Eck’s response with too much cheer and not enough empathy, “That’s because you, well, not just you, but you got here first. You are part of a more completed human mind. There are too many parts your species ignores, from all of your years of survival against predators and the like. Truly a planet of viciousness this one. I realise a lot of this is new, but if you come with me, I can, I can save us both time and let you access the information that is already there." Ooda was stunned, and somewhat dumbfounded by this voice, what was a planet? And what did the spider mean viscous? She had seen many tribe members die at the hands of spider bites, so it was a bit rich this one being so judgemental. As the thoughts prickled the embers of her mind more, the feeling of an expanding awareness threatening to bulge out the sides of her skull, she found herself too curious not to follow.

Detective Peril had already searched the admittedly small number of places in the locked room he was detained in for anything that could help him. The various chemicals, sedatives, and intoxicants which had been forced into his system were still at war with his desire to stay standing and balanced. He flattened his body against the wall and peeked through the steel reinforced glass in the door to get a bearing, or some kind of clue of the facility he might have been held in. As he did so, and pulled his body back to the wall, a waft of a familiar smell was drawn with him, emanating from the space beneath the door. He crouched lower, flaring his nostrils to try to confirm it for himself. It was familiar, but somehow more synthetic, like the smell of flavourings in an artificial cigarette, or some kind of room freshener. The underlying familiarity though, of the purple concoction Peril knew from his own experience of the purple goo from his initiation into the Guidance, and the sachets he had found on members in his recent investigations.

The detective's ponderings were interrupted by the slapping echo sound of footsteps growing in volume towards his door. In what might have been a flash, when sober, in this state, more of a slow blink, the detective threw the cover over the bed, and stashed himself as best his body would allow, under the clothes rail in the wooden cupboard, cracking the door slightly to give a view to the door. It felt like too long for Peril, trying to maintain his balance against the weak chipboard backing of the furniture, until the door clicked open for the off white coated orderly to enter. Luckily for Peril, they seemed all too distracted with headphones and updating a clipboard at the end of the bed with a quick signature, than checking if the occupant was still in the bed. Peril seized the opportunity with a fumbling grasp. Toppling out of the cupboard, barely maintaining his feet beneath him and crashing the orderly into the wall opposite. Peril's comparative size stood in his favour in the short lived tussle with the orderly, his skills in hand to hand combat allowing him, even with a good degree of mental fog, to secure a decent choke hold. After making sure the opponent still had a pulse, Peril grabbed a set of keys from a lanyard now bunched beside the hip of the unconscious orderly. He quickly added the coat onto his own ensemble, pressed the clutch of metal and fobs to the door, and proceeded out, hoping his lack of footwear would not draw attention.

Candi and Chip had managed to slip easily into the lower rooms of the lodge, what had begun as a stooping, foot blade walk, was now more of a casual meandering through the dwelling. The pair had stopped in the security office, beneath the main banquet hall, checking the cameras for any signs of motion, and being rewarded only with the sight of blood stains on the floor of the main banquet room, and two unconscious, possibly dead, members near the main entrance. “I don’t like this at all,” Candi’s voice was stern, as you might imagine from a military commander finding their platoon drunk instead of on watch. “You see those two there Chip?” she continued rhetorically, pointing at the unmoving masses on a screen in the top left of the bank of monitors, “They’re erasers, I heard them talking to each other about it. They’re tough guys, they wouldn’t both get folded by that woman, they couldn’t. I know their partners. We need to see if they’re alright.”. Chip nodded, pleased to not have to control the flow events, “I’m with you Candi, whatever you need. I’m your man, guy, person” he blushed slightly hoping she hadn’t thought he meant boyfriend or partner. "Did you ever think that something like this would happen? That…" Chip was by Candi and her piercing eyes turning to him, "This is a club Chip, for arachnophiles. Yeah there are some lessons taught that are….*beyond what other clubs do* but ultimately, no. I took this as a job, the membership was never in my mind, they offered it to me with options for more flexible working. I would have been crazy to turn that down, the discounts alone can be really helpful…." she trailed off, looking back to the screens, at the blood in the hall, the bodies. "I'm not that fond of all this destiny talk, you know?" she picked up again, "I have never needed to have someone else lay my road out for me, I make my own luck, my own path.". Chip smiled, "That's exactly like a pencil though.". Candi rolled her eyes, "We need to check on those two, and find out what happened in the hall, and whose blood that is."

The security office sat directly beneath the main banqueting hall, so the pair made their way somewhat carefully up the side stairway, hoping to quickly check the cameraless kitchen before investigating the blood and bodies. Chip stacked up willingly behind Candi on their walk up the stairs, enjoying the faint waft of her cassoulette as they ascended. He had been realising with an increasing certainty in her thrall, that she and he were meant for more than just some short scene, they had legs. They were not far from the top, and even with a door between them and the room, they could hear a metallic thudding, like a wooden spoon on pans."What the hell is that?" Chip asked, knowing Candi wouldn't have the answer, but hoping her confident militaristic preparedness may assuage his nervousness. Candi held up a fist like a platoon leader, turning and again pressing a finger to her lips, giving the shut-your-mouth eyes to Chip, which he enjoyed a little too much, smiling and blushing as he obliged. Candi crept further up the stairs to the door, gently releasing the handle and peering round into the stark bright, reflective chrome of the kitchen. There was no visible signs of anyone, and yet, the thuds continued, accompanied by an unintelligible echoed mumble.Candi continued her course, beckoning for Chip to follow, they followed the sound to a chrome cupboard platter stacked on the surface above. The handles to the cupboard had been jammed with several wooden utensils, as they approached, the door appeared to be bending slightly outward from the force applied. "Who's in there?" Candi asked with a pretence of courage and gentle foot kick to the outside of the door. "Get me out of here dammit!" the voice was one Chip recognised, "Chase?" he asked, already pulling the utensils from the handle, "Chase why are you in there?". The folded body of Chase, unfurled himself, with some assistance from his rescuers, from the cupboard. A large section of his face was swollen, and more puce than the reddened frustration of the remainder of it. “Why do you think I am in there you prat?” the furious Chase, having been in the cupboard sometime without help, released his aggression on the nearest target he had. “Its John, and that one from Dale’s birthday.”. Chase quickly went to the fridge, only to find it empty, and inside chugged water straight from the kitchen tap. “I’m going home, tell Jessop, I quit the club, I need a raise or something. I am not dealing with this side of things! I’m the business mind Chip, I am not a fighter, I don’t want violence! Do you understand Chip!?” Chase grabbed Chip's lapels, raising him slightly off the ground, water from the tap still dripping off his chin. Candi placed a hand to his chest, making stern eye contact, immediately diffusing the tension. “You can do one as well Candi, I don’t need this in my life.” Chase dropped Chip, and stormed out of the kitchen, his footsteps disappearing down the corridor, punctuated with a very dramatic slam of the door to the lodge.

“I wonder why he’s so cross?” Chip joked, hoping to lighten the mood, “Candi, your face.”. In the darkness, it couldn’t be seen, but under the invasive brightness of the kitchen lights, it was obvious Candi too would soon have a puce section to match Chase. Chip rounded the end of the kitchen cupboard, and pulled a bag of peas from the freezer, wrapping them in a towel from the countertop before returning, attempting to press them to Candi's face. She took the makeshift ice pack, and motioned him away, she had always found molly coddling of this type uncomfortable. "It won't be my first black eye." She said half laughing, hoping to soften the tension from rejecting his care.

"I know what happened to your "real" police friend." Arachni froze, who was this person? They felt relieved but at the same time more defensive, was this a threat, was this person holding them hostage, had John checked the whole car? "You do?" they said. "I saw him, he was in the lodge, he got taken away on a gurney. I know he's not dead. You were at a cafe and before that a strip club with him. Did you take his car from the cafe?". "Hold the fuck on, I'm interrogating you here." Arachni stopped this stalker in their tracks, they watched him get taken and made no attempt to do anything? "What are you doing here? More importantly, actually, I get why, why you're following us, or me. You're trying to stop this murder spree too. And, your badge" Arachni wobbled the wallet with the identification folded out just far enough toward the ridgedly poised Agent, "How does this have anything to do with the Earth as whole? Do you know about all of this, quantum spider stuff," Klo was felt in the mind of Archni, her displeasure was palpable,"We just need to understand if you want to help us stop them murdering people, or not really. I, this has been an insanely complicated few days for me and there have been dreams, and I shouldn't even tell you. But the thing is. I want to, because everything that has been happening for this entire time, has been driven, pushed, struck, and forced on me, and, and. I need to understand that I have someone other than this maniac" Arachni gestured to the two bites deep in a sandwich, constructed from a variety of the condiments, delicatessen treats, and accoutrements sequestered from the lodge fridge, complete with flatware, John, " who just seems to run into people and puts them unconscious or worse, dead. Tell me, you also know that out of all of this, something, makes sense to you?"

"Is this your first time in a situation like this?" the Agent's condescension, at least as Arachni saw it, was the final straw in a hay of a day, but not as you might imagine, dried in a barn, or swirled in swiss roll slice in a field, but wet, and blown by some great turbine. "Of course it's my v t   first time for the sake of breakfast…. I just really need you to understand, that" Arachni grabbed the taser, set down by the parisian-lunching John, "I will taser you, and, I will get answers." Arachni brandished the taser, not entirely sure how it worked, but hoping the threat was sufficient. They had their finger on what felt like the trigger at least.

"Listen, I, I had a phone" Agent Staff had soiled herself the last three times she had taken taser training, it was a personal goal of hers to control it, but the suit she was in was one of her favourites, and already muddied from the floor, she couldn't imagine having to explain both to a dry cleaner. In the end, this person was willing to share information, and could fill in some blanks from the last few days, she also might have to wear this for some time. John raised herself from a knelt eating position, and wandered forwards; manicured sandwich occasionally pecked at, and fished the phone from Agent Staff's pocket before handing it to Arachni. "What is this about? Unlock it?" Arachni held the phone forwards for Agent Staff to unlock, still holding the taser on her for security. "What am I looking for here?" Arachni asked, staring down at the phone screen. "Play the last video." Agent Sleep suggest-commanded.

It took a few awkward minutes, in the warming morning layby scene for the sandwich finishing John and Arachni to comprehend the vision they had seen. The callous execution of two human beings, as, a performance? That couldn't be their destiny surely? In all of this? What was "part of the journey" about any of what they witnessed? The rubber clad members dragging out the dead. Arachni was so relieved that Peril was alive, and, definitely not a friend of PFM. Equally though, the horror, of the..... Arachni had seen tragic news stories, and the internet was horrific at times, but, the heart piercing pain, of seeing, watching a serial murderer chew through two more people, not in some demonic movie scene of destruction, but a careless click of a trigger. Kidnapping the officer who was investigating him in the first place. It definitely put a dent in Arachni's confidence that John, who was now picking her teeth from the sandwich, and even this Agent, so competent they had lost their weapon and advantage, could do anything to stop PFM.

"OK, OK.....OK......OK" Arachni was stranded in a boot loop for a leadership role they had not expected to be thrust into. This Agent had evidence,"I am Arachni, what is your name?" the only words Arachni could summon to deal with the situation. "Agent Paula Staff, OTES." Paula wiped her hand on her already muddy trousers and offered it to Arachni.

"Oh good," said Eck, spectating the interrogation with Klo from rear window of Peril's car, "It seems we have picked up another recruit, although, I don't know if you saw it Klo, but, she's a bit behind on what's really going on here.". Klo sighed, already knowing what was to be said, but realising Eck was determined to continue with this slow communication style. "What are you talking about now?" she said with tangible frustration. "You really haven't gotten the hang of this yet have you Klo. You wouldn't exactly be doing well here if I wasn't talking you through it, you get so wound up by human communication. You need to see, this is how the humans process things, and we need to guide them, without interfering, slowly lead them. You see, if you tell them exactly in their mind, everything we know, their little brains would melt out of their ears. Also some of them might even try to operate against it, or try to speed things up, and that creates all manner of tangles, particularly with such intricate things such as these. Instead, with their words, their communication style, we must help them to be in the right places. The funny thing being of course, if we do less, they are more likely to be in the right places. You need to learn patience, Klo.". "I know, I just, like you say Eck, I am getting used to this....laid back speed of life." she paused again for a second, trying to practise the pacing,"How are we going to get them to look into the myths without telling them, and stop all of that. They seem more focused on some dead ones.". "Klo, do you not realise who they have just met?" Eck said with surprise. “Of course I do Eck, I am practising slow human processing.”. “Oh very good Klo, very good.”

Peril checked his dulled reflection in the glossy room number sign, glued onto the wall outside, smoothing over his fly away hairs and straightening the clothing so he would look hopefully like just another orderly, minus shoes. He walked with as brisk a pace as his balance would allow, down the longer of the two corridor directions stretching to the left and right outside of his room. It wasn’t a conscious choice, he was in instinct mode, he was following his gut, or whatever pull seemed to drag him the right direction, or in this case maybe the wrong direction, but always to the clue. If you had asked him why, he might have said it was due to the presence of fewer doors, or the blurred sign at the end that might have been an exit or stairs to an exit. Either way, Peril was approaching the first of only three doors in this direction. He stepped wide of the door, trying to hook a glance in through the window, without being observed himself. Through the glass, was an identicate room, with no bedding, and no occupant, so the detective continued his journey. At the second door however; the same glance tactic revealed three people in the room two familiar backs, and one new one, facing the door itself. Peril gave a glance over his shoulder for other orderlies before crouching down against the wall and sliding himself up under the window before peeping through. He could hear a heavily muffled conversation between Lilian and this new person, her familiar smell had seemed to either linger in the corridor or sneak under the door. As Peril lost focus, the new person caught his eye directly. Peril froze, before giving the universally recognised wide-eyed head shake of don't say anything, which this new person seemed to understand instantly. He dropped down from the window and continued off down the corridor. Now was not the time to get caught, and clearly he was not the only person they were keeping here. Where even was here, and why was this new person not sedated like he was? Peril quickened his pace, unsure of whose side this third figure was on.

"I'm just saying," said Agent Staff, having been picked up from the gravel floor next to Peril's car, "that we are likely to attract less attention if we take my SUV than your stolen…"
"Borrowed" John interjected, "Fine, *borrowed,* police car. And besides, mine is made for more terrain types, it's much more functional.". "OK, agreed." said Arachni. "Not agreed," said John, "I don't like to be a passenger.". "What do you mean, we're all following the same lead here John?" Agent Staff was reluctant to leave her SUV in a roadside, and besides, she was the authority in this situation. "Are we?" John, now swinging her

legs on the hood of Peril's car, questioned rhetorically, "I know where Arachni and I have been going. Or where they've been following, or what I've been following." she cocked her head staring out into the woods for a moment. "You could be on a different lead to us, but it just involved the same person. Or something else.". "John has a rumble she follows." Arachni explained the enigmatic half sentences for the puzzled looking Agent Staff, drawing a side eye of derision from John. "So, wait, you don't know why you're even here. I thought the whole reason the Guidance had been chattering about John is she was trying to stop them? But you have no idea at all what you're even doing? You're following a *rumble?*" Staff's voice pitch had rose to a whine by the end of her questions. "It's more complicated than a rumble, it's like the universe moving you, but you can feel the friction as it does." John said defensively; unhappy that the ability, or skill, that had kept her, and others safe so far, was being ridiculed. "I am not disputing whether it exists, or what you feel John. I just, shouldn't we work together? If we are all looking for the same person. Trying to stop the same thing. And wouldn't it be better, to be in my comfortable SUV, than…. well, a car that doesn't belong to you?". John pushed her glasses down and stared over at the SUV for a minute, looking it up and down like a motor trader accessing a junker, or a judge in a bodybuilding contest before ask-telling, “I’m driving?”

As the length left in the corridor Peril had been stalking down shortened, there was a growing smell of the chemically sweet berry that had wafted under Peril’s door earlier. With occasional head turns searching the parallel walls for flickers of shadows approaching, or inward opening doors, he reached the end of the end door, with its sign from up close: “Stairs”; a concept which shook him slightly, but he pressed the clutch of keys again against the new door handle, hearing the click of the mechanism, and giving the hall walls a final detailed perimeter check, before gaining access to it.

After agreeing it was safer to travel in Agent Staff’s, not stolen, or borrowed, OTES issue vehicle, John, Staff, Arachni, Klo and Eck, were travelling to the rumble of John. A rumble which seemed to have produced a deafening effect, judging from the relentless stare she was giving to the road. Barely paying attention to Staff’s wittering about directions of travel. “John, I know we’ve covered this, but I really think we should head back to my offices, we have evidence, this could be reported, we have a case, they could go to jail, or I mean.” John looked for a full 10 seconds, exactly at Staff, full right angle, while staying completely on track on the road, a half smile in the corner of her mouth, which seemed to stop the need for anymore talking about where they were going to. “Why don’t you just upload it to the internet, or put it out there if you’re so concerned,” said Arachni. “Don’t you understand?” Staff replied, craning her head backward into the section between the front seats to address Arachni directly.Shifting her hips round in the seat, legs in a kind of half yoga pose on her lap. “My job is to protect the earth from exposing this all. I know we are partners in this now, I hope, but realistically, I need to speak to you about your future.” she paused sternly, causing Arachni to fish mouth. “You don’t think I noticed Zelon’s in this car too Arachni. This is my job, I , I am a little shocked that you didn’t think I would know about. I….” she trailed off. “It's not going to look good, or help us, if I get the internet staring straight at it all, now is it. Nice to see you again by the way Eck, at least I know it's being taken seriously. And Klo, as well, I just know how important Eck has been to my species but we, already…. this is just for Arachni’s benefit, they don’t seem to catch up quickly in the first instance, that’s all.” Eck and Klo stifled chuckles to themselves. “Ah, well you know me. I never interfere, but sometimes people need to just, a little nudge, maybe, we are ambassadors first you see, a push where you were going anyway, if you think about it.”

Emerging from the long accent of the stairway, in a location he still hadn't come to know, and wondering out into yet another hospital clean doorway, came a calm casual sauntering Peril, still mildly affected by the swirling chemicals in his system. His mind a rush with the themping of his heart in his ears, or, was this sometime else now. He took a less than covert swirling glance around the new corridor space. He still wasn't so sure about the way, but, there was, there had to be something. He decided during this stumbling that, there was a sound to accompany, the noise of the chemical smell entering the detective's nostrils without the need for flared nostrils or sharp inhale. The noise was almost matching what could be his heart still he thought tp himself briefly, before allowing his lead leg to pull his body along the corridor as calmly as he could muster. In part in his mind taking steps to match the sound, in case someone was listening for footsteps. Was it even the day time here? It was the kind, that of swirling clunks and general wetness you can imagine from a beer brewery, or some other distillation process.

"Does anyone have anything to eat?" Arachni asked in the hopes that John hadn't already consumed her walk-in pantry-selection of coat provisions, complete with a bar, and cold savouries.

An Uncertain Void

Ooda had always been different from everyone in her tribe, she noticed when she was quite young, capable of picking up net weaving, and repair, watching her father, by the river estuary. She had tried to introduce an “el” sound to their local dialect, during her teens, in an attempt to add a sense of present dayness to just the activity of “hunt”, but people just thought she had too many fermented berries and had a lazy mouth.

In their small tribe, not too long after a great ice sheet had nearly taken the planet, Ooda was a much more capable member of the tribe. She was key on a hunt, and had developed a hole surrounded by water trapped in stone, which was colder than the outside. Salting and curing, and storing foods so their tribe were never hungry. Some of the skills she displayed were attributed to the forest itself, a daughter of their local god; Nature, protecting them on account of their worship. Never attributed to Ooda herself; she found herself lamenting it too often, but never told anyone.

“Lost?” The noises made by Rai, intelligible to Ooda, were not likely to be understood by a modern English or indeed Spanish, or ancient Mayan speaker. “Forbidden tree, not far. Don’t Listen, if no mouth!” the warning given by Fera, uttered and mimed by Ooda, trying to remain quiet, in case they could add to their list of fertile territories.

It was late in the day, the sun sliced through the trees, the angle giving the light a green tinge through the thickness of the forest. Ooda had pushed them deeper than they would usually go, she wasn’t sure why, but knew there was something better going deeper. It was only the two of them now, most had gone home, happy with the day’s successes, and getting low on water.

“Rai?” Ooda muttered softly, having been distracted by the low lights across the forest. They never were never in the forest this deep with this kind of light in the day. “Where are you?”. At some point in her perimeter sweep of this evening verdancy, he must have wandered off? The thought held in her mind optimistically. They were never here this late. “Rai?!”

Scrunching the note from the door into her pocket, John heaved open the surprisingly well hinged, oak door. Out through the stale smell of the doormat in the smaller porch, onto the wider decked porch, down the steps, and towards the haphazardly parked cars outside. “Wait a minute John,” Arachni blurted while trying to catch the now swingin closed door, “Where are you going? Where are we going?”. John paused for a second, before turning on her heel, “You’re right,” she said, striding back towards the door, “Provisions.” her glasses masking her eyes as she smiled sweetly, moving past Arachni, who had now been pressed into the door to make way for John's return.

Arachni followed John’s biker boots which were making a dull thudding along the wooden floor with each purposeful stride, through the house to the kitchen, where the tone switched with the transition to tiles.

As Arachni rounded the corner, from the hall into the kitchen, they were met with the sight of John using her forearm to clear shelves of the fridge. Scooping into the strangely elasticating inside pocket of her jacket, meats and vegetables, condiments, and platters of h'orderves; presumably from a previous club party. There didn't seem to be any sound though of their fate inside the pocket, no shatter as glass beer bottles toppled in with equally vulnerable glass condiment jars. " Provisions." John announced on Arachni's arrival, with the prideful lip curls of a soldier preparing their kit for battle; pleased with their perceived readiness. "What's with your coat John? And, honestly, can you stop for just a second and explain to me. What are we doing?" Arachni's voice raised with frustration. "There was blood in that room, and do you know that one of those cars out front belongs to a police officer?!" Arachni's voice rising further with each dangling and dangerous thread of their situation. "He was a good person, what if it's his?!" John by this point had moved to the cupboards and was trying but failing, to tactfully continue placing individual cans into her pocket, maintaining the head position for eye contact, behind the shaded protection of her glasses."These people are murderers..and," Arachni boiled over to a vented simmer," you're prepping dinner?!".

"Is this your first time?" John had taken all the food she needed from the cupboards, and now hung her thumbs inside the edges of those same pockets. Arachni's thoughts wandered for a moment as she scanned John's posture. What would happen if she put her thumb all the way in the pocket? Would she lose it? Would it stretch?

“My first time?” Arachni replied with spines, “My first time with murder happening, everywhere, apparently, and no police to speak of?...Yeah!”. “Well, this is not my first time seeing this.” John's calm reply delivered like a salve to the prickles, “You have been cast, by whatever it is that weaves these things. You do not choose it, it didn’t even choose you, it just is. And you know what?” John paused and lent forward on the kitchen island in the middle, dropping her tone to an ominous whisper of secret truths to be revealed. “It’s far better …..to just always have some food on you.” She lent back against the counter behind her, adding “I even get to give some away to people who need it.” She folded her arms defiantly, as though closing the argument.

“That is not the problem here John!” Arachni let loose after letting John’s complete missing of the point get to them.”Aren’t you afraid of the consequences of this? Of police? Prison? What if we die?”. “Well, of course we’re going to die,” said John with a matter of factness that irked Arachni, “Everyone dies.”. “Don’t be facetious, this is real, there’s blood! In the next room John?” Arachni’s vocal expressions had moved from irate to incredulous, a little shaken with relief from the release. “Like I said, this isn’t my first time.” John’s reply with a slight smile in the corner of her mouth. “You can choose to run away from things or towards things, but there’s going to be things, sometimes like this, sometimes better. But sure as anything, you’ll die in the end. Gotta at least enjoy yourself, or not fight the tide, or fight it all you want. We are in this story, this series of events, and you just.... don’t want to be hungry on top.....or thirsty.” She chuckled and fished a beer bottle from her pocket, removing the cap with leverage from a knife on the drying rack of the sink beside her. “Are you high?” Arachni blurted. “Not yet,” said John, “Look,” she brought her voice to a less flippant register. “I don’t want to say what will happen, because I don’t know, but I’ve not run into police around these guys. I don’t know, I guess they’re in it, or they can use what this guy already did on those people in the diner. I have no clue. I told you, I will follow the rumble.You got to find your own way to go with it you know?”. “You saw what happened in the diner?” Arachni’s question held out as a dual enquiry on how long John had been watching them.

The room was the temperature it was supposed to be, a soft mattress, on fresh sheets, the smell of the detergent, like a kind of safety; waking up the Detective, the crook of his elbow aching slightly, the cold steel of an ankle cuff confirming to him the situation. At the end of the bed, merging into individual focus, a willowy woman, of indeterminate age, and the second figure; a shock of yellow, atop a purple face.

"Lilian?" the detective groaned out the greeting half question to the slowly materialising, attractively familiar, willowy woman standing at the foot of his bed. He had woken up with more painful hangovers, but this was the most coagulated his thoughts had felt in a good few years. How long had it been since the night at the club? It seemed like the room had a bright window, but he couldn't make out anything through it. His mind drifted to the pain in his elbow pit and wondered whether this was more than a standard IV, he would have to pull it out when they weren't looking. "You said, you'dn't take part in this stuff?" his best attempt at a comedy-casual question, formed with a mouth that wasn't as complicit as he'd have liked, considering the company.

Peril tried to shuffle his body up onto the pillows behind him, hoping to mask his arm movements and continued in spite of his impedance "You…, this is all boys club sbloney, you said, you said medicine. Are you?". The detective fell deeper into the pillows behind, unable to support his head on his neck, or self on his elbows. That same willowy. and familiar outline drew herself closer to the detective. “But, I am in medicine Folsy. How do you think you made it here in one piece?” her voice gentle as Folsom had ever remembered it, asked rhetorically. “You are in the way of something important we are building. Like you always were I guess. Jessop and I, we were looking at the compound you took in the trees. It’s… unbelievable the things we can do with this knowledge. Oh Folsy, if we could get everyone to understand, the good it does so you can connect your mind." Her voice mirrored the kinetic type of excitement the detective recalled in Jessop from that day in the great tree. “People would live stronger, longer lives, fewer health problems even at age, and then…. But you already know all this don’t you? ” her voice trailed off as she adjusted the covers up on the bed, shifting a small piece of hair from his slowly close fluttering eyes.” I can keep you safe here. It was meant to happen like this, don’t you see?” her final rhetoric echoed into the detective's thoughts, as he slipped back into welcoming blackness.

Agent Staff had been a part of the Earth’s Suppression Outreach Team, or ESOT, sometimes OTES for obscurity reasons, for over 8 years, and was as dedicated an agent as any other. It was a prestigious organisation, or held itself as one, with many rebrandings over the years to reach the perfect in ambiguous titles for a branch of planetary governance. Their task, to keep all of the humans focused on planet Earth, its future, and misdirected from access to information that the species was not ready for, as a whole; or at least, this was the doctrine the Agent subscribed to. It would be like handing machine guns, with armour piercing bullet technologies, to mediaeval knights; a quote from a superior which Staff had felt resonated perfectly with her mistrust in the population's ability to do, what she believed, were, the right things.

Taking long strides for her height and in sensibly rugged combat boots, which did not match the rest of her well pressed suit, Agent Staff strode across the wide country road between the tree banks, searching the road both ways for traffic, but none was in earshot. Her destination, on a small roadside, encircled with more tall redwood trees, the OTES issued SUV. There were no identifiers of its authority fleet status, no lights on top, crests, coats of arms, or badges, just the metallic green paint and the fact she didn't have to pay for the fuel; which was a plus.

As she moved across the empty roadside to the car, her hands shook in her pockets, she clutched the phone in the right outside jacket pocket as though it might break out and rampage across a nation. Agent Staff had been on the trail of one of the biggest corruptions in her particular branch of governing in living memory, she had a witness willing to testify waiting in the car, and had just taken video of an execution. Not in the dark and ominous way that it sounded, but an unfolding of a horrific chain of events that, in its sinister way, she needed. She was finally ready to take this up the chain, to wipe the smirks from the faces of her colleagues who told her not to worry about this organisation. "They've been around forever Paula," Agent Staff recalled the condescension of her area leader, when she had said she was going to the lodge to investigate the links to the groups leader. "It's just coincidence, trust me, we wasted a lot of resources on them before. It was before your time but trust me. Many better representatives have been caught up, trying to be the police. We are not, I repeat, not the police. We can detain, in serious circumstances, but come on, take it to the police if you are worried about missing persons. As far as I can see there are no credible reports of them doing anything to commit to a mass reveal. Our job, spin, obfuscate, and if it's bad, wipe em. And you seem hellbent on getting to being a toast burning, wannabe detective officer again. The Guidance *are* with us.". Well, Agent Paula was feeling both vindicated, and shaken to her core, as though her investigation was coming to a close, but she had only scratched the surface it seemed, she had never felt more in danger. As her fingers reached under the door handle, she cast her eyes around the emptiness of the car parking area, before looking through the car window and noticed something was wrong. Where was the witness?

The sun had long since left the sky when Agent Paula Staff and her star testimony had crunched into the layby in the now empty SUV. “Chip, I’m going to need you to stay in the vehicle for me, while I scout ahead on this. According to my map, the lodge should be just through here.” her gaze locked to the tree line opposite,”... and you said the whole back window is glass?” She turned her head back toward Chip but didn’t need a reply, but was awarded a nod.”That should help things.” The agent ran through her plan not really to Chip, but to herself, as she usually did in her head before any major meeting, although this was not like her usual investigations, she couldn’t risk memories being wiped here. What are the key points, how do I deliver them; she was preparing, this was the one.

“You know this could get quite serious, if they succeed, they might take away my role in the administration,” Eck had been pining self importantly to Klo on the porch for at least long enough for it to become tiresome, since John and Arachni had disappeared into the house for provisions."Not just for me though, if they have records of it ALL, I mean some of it is very familiar to the eternal myth." Eck's half sentences half questions to the wind, were getting frantic. "What are you talking about Eck, sometimes, sometimes, I think you should just take your own advice, and not interfere." Klo tried to stem the flow of introspective concern spouting from Eck."You didn't assume to be in your current position, but, you are there, as sure as you will be somewhere else.". "Don't patronise me Klo, I am a Galactic ambassador. I'm just concerned, what if our myths and their myths combine? Or. Human beings are so few. Who would have thought they could get themselves together like this. They always seemed so isolated."

Ooda had been searching for Rai for too long; the thought in her mind, as she saw the shadows of the trees starting to swaddle the leaves and branches into a violet moss around her. Finding a way back would be treacherous. "Rai," Ooda softly muttered across the dark, her eyes expertly strafing the undergrowth for protruding limbs, or the ovaled eyes of four legged predators. It was the lack of sound entirely that put Ooda into a sense of unrest, why wouldn't he answer? The forest was never quiet, not at this time of day?

Then, almost as if exactly timed, Ooda recognised a gentle murmuring coming from the otherside of a particularly thick tree trunk and lower canopy. She brushed it aside and emerged almost as if through a waterfall of foliage into an open hoof shape. Or it felt like it. It stretched around and out of Ooda's peripheral vision, in the middle, stumble-running horizontally across her sightline, disappearing on the right and reappearing on the left, the muttering Rai, smiling a helpless, exhausted smile but not stopping. "Rai, what do?". Rai disappeared into a point and reappeared again, in the distance, from the other end, still half running, a clutch of purple berries in his left hand, leaking into his fingers. "Stay!" Ooda moved across the cooling evening, the sun bending a thin odd-pinked orange arch with edges of the navy rising night spreading to the edges of the treelines, like the inside of the rolled leafs smoked on special occasions, but without the materials inside. The hollowed inside of a spear, but more beautiful. She grabbed Rai by the top of his forearm as he approached her intercepting perpendicular track, Ooda squatted down into the immaculate grass, bringing him to a stop with her motion. Rai smiled a purple tinged grimace gratefully, before toppling onto his side. "What?" Ooda asked again at Rai, who was gulping air like water for thirst. Rai muttered meekly, "No talk, No Mouth".

As the sun traced down the sky, in a park, behind a hut, that seemed a long time ago now, Chip Winner's eyes fluttered into focus on the outline of a suited woman, with silver aviators; the trees and blurred concussion had robbed his vision of any further study."You're awake," her captioning helping Chip into the situation, "I notice your coat, and of course," she paused raising her head toward the hut, "the location we are, are you a member?". Chip recalled his mandatory induction, and the protocol in case the society was about to be revealed."I'm just a citizen lost in the woods. I must have fallen over." Chip knew he'd made a fine job of that nonchalant response as he concussidedly half smiled at the now tilting shadow of Agent Staff. "Yes," she cut through this blatant lie, "My name is Agent Staff, or Paula, I understand you know this man?" she placed between her body and Chip's face, her phone screen, brightness to full; the all too unique side profile of Jessop was clear as day to Chip.

As John strode out of the kitchen and back into the familiar boot thuds on the wooden floor, she continued, "You said you wanted to know where we go next, well, help us out, I have to go, if you have to go too, then something should just... you know?". She flicked her wrists and shoulders up to the sky with the flourish of *I-don't-know-what-to-tell-you*, "Does anything stick out to you here, are you feeling drawn in any direction?". "What do you mean drawn in a direction?" Arachni blurted in what was becoming a more familiar tone when dealing with John. "I don't have a rumble John, I'm not a game controller, I don't." they trailed off to a more even temper. "This is something I am getting used to, and your lack of specificity is starting to get to me." . "Have you even tried?" John asked, shaking her head before the answer could be made. Arachni cast a gaze around the walls and the facets on the circular vaulted ceiling of the entrance foyer. At first, running across paintings, parchments behind glass, small tools from early civilizations on display, each with some spider like design. Some of them in glass cabinets, but by the door, there, an ornate bowl; as a result of distance, it appeared like wide-set wicker, but closer to, as Arachni approached, was a wood carved, webbed bowl, complete with its own three dimensional long limbed spiders, separating keys. A set that flashed into Arachni's mind from under the hand of a spider candied sleeve, in a diner a few events ago now, suddenly almost pulled their hand out toward it. Arachni held the keys out to John as if they were the answer to her question in its action, but clarified. "We're going to need a car.". John smiled, "You sound like a wally, throw them here let's go.". "What?, I was drawn to them." Arachni protested feeling robbed of what felt like the first time they had some feeling of control on events and threw them to John. “Well, yes you were drawn to them, but that doesn’t mean you get it yet.” John pulled the front door to the lodge and activated the unlocking clunk flash of Perils car while doing so.

“They’re quite dramatic these ones,” Eck commented as Klo appeared next to him on the parcel rack of Peril’s automobile. “What do you mean dramatic?” asked Klo, knowing there was no choice in the matter but to indulge him. “Well,” returned Eck, triumphant in his bluster, “They spend such a long time bickering and chattering about things, and not a lot actually doing things. I said to John, one of the reasons she is a familiar of mine is her ability to just do. You know, less of this, I will, I shall, should we shouldn’t we, which can hold people to apathy.”. “You enjoy conversation in this realm though don't you?” Klo was still not accustomed to the leisurely pace at which most humans interacted, and considered whether Eck was trying to train her in endurance."Oh very much so yes, they do offer the ability to spread a thought over a little longer a space than otherwise might have been given to it. I wonder to myself often on days like this, on the warmth of this ground, in the relative safety of our existence, now, at least as we see it, bound in this set of events, whether we are wrong to see it as beneath us. Perhaps, maybe we can lose ourselves in infinity, in the ever lost feeling of anything, and can't see the now, but the now is everything for these things, and somehow. Should we not tell them, I worry that by asking it might stir up their desire to know more, and then it might lead them to it anyway." "Are you talking about these prison records?" Klo asked impatiently, "Do they even realise how close this could all get to being a big mess? Sometimes I watch it and wonder? But it never hit us Klo, this could change everything for us, this could break things I don't even understand. And I have a very long existence area, deep, wide, and varied." He puffed himself up into the sun beams streaking the parcel shelf of the warm dust moted car. "When do we need to worry?" asked Klo, feeling a little more concerned than before. Eck deflated slightly, and muttered "Now.".

"Look, all you have to do is be ready," John continued her sermon to Arachni as they both dropped themselves to the butt into the leather upholstered seats of Detective Perils voiture. "I don't mean the sky is falling yet you see Klo, I am just telling you, you need to be ready," Eck tried to assuage the concern he could feel emanating from Klo. It seemed to shake his physicality like the car engine as it turned over, bone rattling the car into ignition. “So all we need are snacks then, and a car?” Arachni sarcastically asked the already non sarcastically, affirmatively nodding John. “It is the most you can prepare yourself in my experience,” John reaffirmed her point, pulling the car out from the long gravel and bark crushed driveway away from the lodge and out onto the main road. “So how are we supposed to prepare for this, whilst not involving ourselves?” Klo asked Eck as the sun trilled its branch shaded fingers across the parcel shelf. “Well, we need to get all of the information first of course,” Eck tried to bluff, “Once we know, then we will know what we have to do.”. “I thought you said you knew what you were doing though?” Arachni queried John’s unwaveringly confident forward stare into the road beyond. “Well, once things are more clear, I can see a way through, but at the moment, we just need to make sure there is enough food, for when we don’t know what to do?” John reached into a side pocket, fishing out a carton of grapefruit juice, pouring it deftly, with only a minor glance for accuracy, into a plastic tub, taped onto the parcel rack. “You see,” Eck said, moving to the fresh poured grapefruit juice, “John is prepared, and we are fine. Sometimes,” he gulped and continued with satisfaction, “I think we have to trust these humans have this covered.”. Klo couldn’t pull the kind of expression Arachni might have in this situation, but the feeling inside was equivalent to incredulous, existence questioning, wonder. As though the leader of a nation had told you war was to be determined on the outcome of a game of rock, paper, scissors, between two chickens.

“Let’s try this again,” sighed Agent Staff, as any bemused enforcement officer might, as she helped Chip to his feet. He was swaying slightly with an arm and hand buttress supporting the head. “I know you are with the Guidance, I saw you enter an interdimensional storage area, without any concern for passers-bys, who were uninformed. You could have caused an incident.” She lowered her glasses and could see Chip's glazed focus following very little of what was being said. “ I need to speak to this man” She brandished the phone screen at his face for a second time.”You know him as a, Brother Jessop” Agent Staff maintained a wary eye on Chip, who still would not have made a great escape on the legs beneath him at that time, while she scooped up some keys and other detritus that had somehow left Chips person, she knew how they had left, but would not be pursuing anything just yet. ”I think you should come with me,” Agent Staff hooked under Chip's arm and helped him to wander back out to parks waning light.

“I just joined ‘cos the weather 6 guy joined one,” Chip half slurred, ”I never thought it’d go like this you know.” After a few minutes of Agent Staff's no nonsense striding through the nightfall cooling park, Chip seemed to believe he had been caught by the police, and was now in a full confession mode, making sure he distanced himself as much as possible from any potential for recrimination in the future. Of course, due to his current cognitive function, it sounded more like the apologetic football player, caught taking an illegal stimulant, and now has to make a public apology, but they actually were a good person, and it disappointed their mum, which made her cry, and makes them cry on top because they just wanted to make her proud. " I haven't even been in long, and I can help you, they're having a meeting, it's something big, and they're all going to be there. I can show you. I don't know if I can be." Chip hoped that his performance was working, he needed to figure out a way to get a message to Jessop that OTES were coming.

Chip purposefully made a meal of his injuries the entire way back to the car, trying to keep this authority, which one was this, he wasn't sure but he needed to get to a phone."Am I in custard?" Chip asked faux-sorrowfully, "No, we just need to understand a few things that have been happening here. What happened to the third man that entered with you, for instance?" the Agent paused glancing across Chips frosted dull eyes, "It seems as though you need medical attention, so we will get you feeling steady first, then deal with what you have been doing." The Agent quickened her pace and the pair arrived at the OTES SUV only too soon for Chip, who was only now beginning to realise how this concussion was muddling his mind. Was this the police? "Am I the rest?" Chip asked again, trying to embellish his condition but genuinely struggling with mouth movement beyond a slur."Almost there Mr Winner, you mentioned a lodge we were going to?" Agent Staff thought she might try her luck, although not strictly ethical, this was a lead too good to pass, something inside her told her, even though she was not usually one to thumb the scales; it had to happen this way. "Oh yes, it doesn't really have an address you know. I have, there's a link on my, I'll show you, do you have a map in your phone?".

As Chip softly closed the car door, still feeling somewhat muddy in the mind from earlier, he wondered if this betrayal of Agent Staff's kind nature might be a problem in the future. It didn't matter, this was a chance to be something, to seize a chance to something. He knew he was more than just an attractive weatherman, he was integral, a main thread, in how the world discovered. Everything. He had guided the Agent to the layby perfectly, he knew the area well as a back entrance to the lodge for extra curricular activities with some of the more attractive members. A little further up the road there was a simple wooden gate entrance to the reflection garden, from there he could get to the house.

It must have been over 20 minutes since Agent Staff had left Chip thought to himself alone; lent against the cold car side panel, he knew he could make it to the other side of the road without an issue. Chip stoop-ran across the road, just out of precaution, scrambling in smart shoes up the mudded embankment and down into the woodland area behind the lodge's maintained garden, but still on the land. As he caught himself on the trunk of a tree for balance, he could make out, facedown in the mud, and in that familiar blazer, a few trees in the distance, ahead in a clearing, Candi from security detail. Chip thought about stopping, but wasn't sure if he had the time to waste. He managed to send a quick text to Jessop from the Agent's phone while they were in the park, pretending to struggle with using the mapp app to find the destination. A feat he was feeling much more proud of considering his current rising nausea. Chip strode along the more beaten mudded path in the wood to the rear door of the reflection Garden, and could soon make out from the vantage point, the grand dining hall window, hidden under the sill beneath was a crouched Arachni, and equally foetal positioned John from the security email. Chip slowly backed out of the reflecting garden, trying carefully, but failing utterly, not to trip the security light.

Only a few hundred metres away from Chip, poised behind a moss dampened, and fallen log, Agent Staff had her phone trained on the Panoramic back window of the lodge, like a wooden bezeled television. This is unbelievable she thought, steadying her tremor from the adrenaline, this is not just a disappearance, a suicide, some other non culpable act. She saw, she had recorded, in, was it bits, or electrical charge, there was evidence, clear, people died. There was an officer, she recognised him from before, how is this all coming together. And why do these two keep showing up everywhere? Particularly John, she was meant to be a rumour. As her mind klaxoned with anxiety bells, and fear, neurologically flushed with chemicals, there was a small flash of a security light and the click of a garden gate. Did they know she was here? Staff was not going to wait around and risk not being vindicated, or worse executed like she had just witnessed. She pocketed the phone tremulously, keeping her hand pressed to it so it wouldn't, couldn't, escape the coat pocket, as she stalked her way on a retreat arc from the scene of the crime.

Lilian Pad, was at maximum stride as she lent back in her chair, everything was coming together, something not even Jessop could foresee, so lost in his vision to supplement himself to blindness. She allowed her gaze to drift out of the floor to ceiling arched window, the sun overcast by cloud on an otherwise clear sky, far to the harbour city in the distance, it's glistening waters beyond, and closer, to a steep and crisp pine gradient, out again to a more deciduous forest below, between her, and the traffic, the noise, and the people. When Jessop came to her 18 months ago with a vision, she had already been on a journey of her own. even further than edges of the water as it somehow didn't quite touch the sky, but lapped its edges.

"Professor Grehnikin, and Dr Pad, what is your intention here?" the customers officer at border control asked, seeming not to check their faces from behind darkened glasses, a necessity in the bright white room. "We are here on a mission of discovery," Lil was almost too excited, and drew honest scrutiny from the officer who would normally not have paid much attention to two, well, he might call them "science types". This kind of nervous uneasiness on the feet of this woman as she seemed to be rolling back and forth on her feet, was what he would expect from someone with something to hide, but these cases were chrome, locked and sealed, with tapes of varying complexity. Just to open it could take an afternoon of international calls, conversations with Jenny the interpreter, and things had been awkward there for too long, a whole afternoon with her, no, in the end, they seemed to check out. “We have papers from Biotyme if its assistive in any way? We have a schedule to keep, we should have been there last week.” Lilian excitedly, effervesced, she was hoping the enthusiasm might detract from any notion from this border officer to check the contents of their baggage. Not that there was anything to hide, but just the time to go through it all, for the third time on this transit. “The weather in this region though, so unpredictable at times.” Lilian continued to witter to the guard, she had entered countries as a scientist thousands of times in her career, with samples and without, with equipment, and without, but this had been the most fraught with checks, every border seeming to have an issue with her passing. Perhaps it was the presence of Grehnikin. She wondered if this was a sign of things to come, or if this was just the culmination of probabilities from journeys unchecked. “I’ve never had problems before this,” Lillian hissed out of the corner of her mouth to Grehnikin, “It must be you, what have you been up to, are we going to have to explain all this? Again?”. “I thought you liked talking about our work?” Professor Grehnikin, casual and calm as ever, turning with a quarter smile of smoulder to Lilian. instantly diffusing her anxiety countdown. " We have to the hotel here anyway, it's too late to start out yet. What's wrong with another keynote address, and then maybe something relaxed, in the bar," He cast his eyes and head around dramatically continuing, " I hope they have." Grehnikin always had that flippant attitude to any situation, as though danger was just an appointment to be kept endured and moved past, an amuse bouche for a cocktail. It was what had drawn Lilian too close in the past, but that charm would be essential in finding some of these villages, which were too far off of any track, to have ever feared a beating. They grabbed the chromed handles to the heavy corrugated, wheeled cases, and shepherded them through the security boundaries, and following Grehnikin's keen identification, across the tiled concourse, to the ubiquitous airport bar. Even without the seminar on their gear, both travellers were ready for anaesthetic.

Lilian lent on her palm, allowing her cheek to smoosh up into her temple area. They spent months trekking the forest, speaking with locals, learning new dialects not even recorded, trading information for help, for supplies.They had claimed to be on a fact finder for Biotyme, a company that Lilian had been a senior project lead in new biochemical process designs for. They were going to source some of the original berries, berries Lilian remembered from University days, with her favourite professor Grehnikin, berries that could only be sourced, according to the professor, in a remote part of the Amazonian rainforest. The plan for Biotyme, was to cross engineer it, with a more hardy plant to produce the berries in a less challenging environment to cultivate. Some simple gene splicing, or maybe husbandry, and it would be resolved, the potential for profit was limitless, and these could genuinely help people, Lilian had assured the head of the grant committee of it.

The truth though, Lilian knew the future, it was not going to be a supplement, the grand awakening that Jessop wanted, with the intrinsic deaths that accompany a mass april foolsing like that. When you pull the rug out, someone is bound to bump their heads on the edge of the fireplace and die. Somehow though Jessop believes this number will be low, but imagine the unrest, when they see how stagnant we have been. No, the way of taking the lead over people was never going to be the way, not in Lilians heart, she just wasn't paying attention to the humans to begin with. And while she wasn’t paying attention, she picked up a few friends from other planets, who had their own stories to distract from the world at large. It was in this assimilation of information on a grand scale that sewed the seeds of the only future Lilian could believe in. An ancient power, bound, the great unravelling. No more would humans be bound to Zelon futures, but free, to construct their own interweavings.

As she felt her mind truly dissolving through the window into the outside, the warmth of the now emerged sunshine on her face welcoming her to answers of the future, a glass timbre knock announced the presence of Jessop outside her door. “We have another guest to visit.” his statement, more command than request, but Lil was happy to oblige, she had some questions of her own.

Fumbling the cool, painted metal door bolt closed on the garden, Chip took a moment for his eyes to adjust again to the darkness. If John was here,he thought to himself, he needed protection, this wasn’t a straightforward warning of police, this could be a rescue mission, or even a stand alone story, of taking the lead. Being a leader, and being strong. Chip wasn’t sure, but as his eyes scanned the darkness for foot placements, his thoughts swept his mind for ideas, and quickly settled, that Candi, ex-champion fighter Candi, would be able to shoulder the difficult parts, while he would still be there, in the end, a name in the books. He picked his way back through the increasingly less manicured woodland, towards the spot he had seen her last, planking a mud puddle.

As Chip approached the area he remembered her being in, he found a sight he had not thought of as being so beautiful before. Crouched against a tree, checking with her finger and phone camera, with torch full beam for missing teeth; of which there were none in this digit wrangled smile, the mud streaked face, of Candi. “Candi,” Chips whisper-shouted through the trees, incase they weren’t alone, jerked attention, and an index finger, from Candi’s mouth. “It’s Chip, from the founders fondue, do, I was, I wasn’t very fond of ew, cheese, it was ….a joke, you were…. Are you ok?” Chips garbled anecdotal identification was enough for Candi to relax her shoulders, she recalled his clumsy conversationalism, she also was confident that she did not have to seek any dental assistance. “What are you doing here? John is on site,” Candi quickly slipped into a security and debrief mindset. ” I tried to intervene,” she touched briefly the red-purpling side of her face that had received the impact, “Guess I got lucky, she moved my mouth guard though, so I wouldn’t choke, that’s…., the notes mentioned security risk.” Candi lost her focus a little, possibly from the injury, but possibly on the thought that maybe John wasn’t what she had been led to believe. “I am fine,” she continued recalling Chip’s, until then, unanswered query, “I didn’t know you were in the lodge, are you ok?”. “I wasn’t, truth be told Candi, I was caught by some OTES agency trying to silence us, and, I mean I let Jessop know by text, but,” Chip turned his head gravely to the halo of light in the direction of the lodge “Candi,” he hardened his tone, “We need to get in there,” he motioned with clasped finger guns, “You mentioned John was on site. I thought that she was taken care of in that diner, I mean I sent two good guys.” he allowed himself to trail off, in plastic memorial, “We have to save everything, this could be, this could be, the world, at stake Candi?” The last few words held with pause in hope of inducing a feeling of magnitude. She looked at him incredulously, he seemed oblivious to her recuperation from the last encounter with John. “I think I am going to wait here then,” Candi responded flatly, “If there are police or authorities, I am not getting myself arrested, or worse losing teeth over this. Come on Chip, it's a club for the sake of breakfast.” Chip looked blankly for second at her; puzzled with the word choice, “Candi, this isn’t just a club, I know you have not been privy to some of the deeper truths we can offer here, but people could be hurt,” he paused again hoping to summon some sense of occasion from its space,”You, you are their protection, I know this doesn’t happen often, but when it does. Don’t you, owe it, to the honour of the position, to rise up and…”. “Why are you not doing it then?" Candi cut across quickly, well aware of this tactic, "If it is so noble, why aren't you running in to save the day.". "Candi, beautiful, MMA Champion, Candi, athletic, skilled in this kind of scenario Candi. Or just me, I mean I lift, we all know I can move if I have to, I just, some people are just…." Chip produced from his pocket an elegant fountain pen, which elicited Candi to mimic his action, producing her own pencil from inside her blazer. "Do you even understand what it is that you are Candi? This is more than just a symbol, you are capable of drawing and erasing, changing the very lines of our fate. And anyway aren't you supposed to love this fighting stuff. It's not just to give you that phenomenal figure is it?" Chip smoulder-smiled the last of his barrage of hopefully subtle enough, ego boosting, commentary to initiate the response he needed from Candi. I mean, no one was expecting him to go in by himself, and risk losing the knowledge of the, the books and all of the, he was very important to the organisation….. as an arbiter, advertisement for member benefits. Death would not be a benefit even he could sell.

A long way away from the tribulations of Chip and his task to be an expert convincer, Agent Sleep had been trying to figure a way out. Only two days ago, or at least he hoped that long ago, he had been outside of a diner with his partner at OTES Paula. He was just trying to humour her tin foil ramblings, but was sure of their tin nature no longer. “Seriously Sleepy, this is is a genuine exposure plot that could actually succeed, we need to do something about it.” Sleep recalled Staff tirading for the third time in their monthly briefings about these leads. He was just indulging a theory, he never genuinely thought things could end up, wherever this was. The room he had awoken in only a day ago was the kind that you might expect from a high end, self catering, holiday flat, rental. The bedding and fixtures were just high enough quality to give the illusion of quality that was profitable from visitors only selecting based on image quality in an app. He didn’t feel like he was being held in a prison, but certainly this would not be a homely feel to a room either, this wasn’t the bedroom of a house. The door had security netted glass, and was locked from the outside.

He and Agent Staff, or at he had, been what expected a routine clean up on an exposure event. Apparently some diners had witnessed a breakdown of a disciple of the eternal and unfathomable. These things happen. It was not uncommon in their line of work, many disclosure attempts involved people who had come to understand, or at least to perceive, from their perspective at best, how much of a puppet of fate they were; they felt compelled to forever cut, any strings, to anyone or any act, not realising the act itself, of cutting the strings, was the act of the string twichers, the endless undulation of time, rippling decision and action of millions. There is no escape it just is. This incident though, it seemed, or at least from the information they had managed to obtain, that nonone actually saw it anyway. There had been footage on a phone, which was mostly contained, spun into obscurity, and welded tin helmets, on any sites it existed on. This was important. Agent Sleep was a firm believer that people, the population, had not yet learned to share well enough, to share the knowledge that they had not yet been given the opportunity to grasp, not in any structured educationally standardised way.The knowledge that could corrupt as well as it could encourage, that could be used for the quick ends of profit, for the self, rather than benefit of all.

Agent Staff had peeled off to follow an alternative looking suspect with a rucksack, Paula was curious why there seemed to already be a detective on the case to begin with, only to discover that this person was not associated with OTES at all. Staff had always been headstrong in following her instincts and being honest. Agent Sleep, in a similarly instinctual sense, had not been able to follow his normal morning ablutions schedule, and was now very much out of sync, and uncomfortable. He took the opportunity to take this time alone to have a comfort break, in the diner's pleasantly hygienic facilities perhaps he could get his head round where this might be going. It couldn't be as serious as Staff was making out, but still, it was a peculiar event, surrounded in peculiarity.

He couldn't have taken more than five minutes to complete his leavings, but thereafter his timeline becomes muddled, until the waking in this room. He wasn't sure if he ever left the commode itself, but definitely had distinct memories of sunshine in his eyes; the swing-click of the door closing behind him. Had he been struck on the head? He allowed his right hand to fingertip-graze over the contours of his skull, but finding no lumps, or unrecogised one, contusions, or crusted scabs. He couldn't place how he had got here, was Agent Staff in trouble? Why could he not recall any details either. He knew he had to focus on resolving his own situation first before resorting to any rescue attempts on as yet, unconfirmed kidnapees. Where was this? He strode halfway to the window, only to identify in closer focus that it was not the outside, the beautiful video image of an outside, water and mountains, presumably somewhere, maybe somewhere here? But not there, not that space, where there was no window. As the realisation set in, almost in serendipitous sympathy, the door lock and handle clicked open, revealing with its soft swing, the purple faced man from the other day, and a willowy looking scientist that Agent Sleep was not familiar with, before clicking closed.

"If you're so prepared, why didn't you think to go before we left in the car then John?" Arachni scolded John, as this was the only refutable evidence of a lack of preparedness she had displayed since their meeting. "You couldn't have included toilet's in your provisions?". John side eyed Arachni as they pulled in to a layby, knowing she was just following the rumble, that ultimately, she had to follow the machinations of the story, there was no choice, it was when it was time. As the tyres popped and scrunched in declaration of their arrival, John's focus was pulled to the unexpected presence of another vehicle, strangely early, definitely not a hunter, considering the lack of bumper stickers, dents, scuffs, or gun rack. As the car crawled to a stop, Arachni had given in to the situation, accepting the sounding off as venting stress akin to an inmate at their prison guard. Ultimately, they were there for the duration, better learn to adapt. John quickly unbuckled, swept out of the car; closing the door with equal efficiency, and was soon scrambled over the embankment which marked the edge of the car area of the layby, into the undergrowth, to find a secluded spot. As the door closed, Arachni realised they had been awake too long, and asleep too little. Perhaps a moment or two, just to look at the eyelids.

Since hearing the sound of an engine rumbling up the road, Agent Staff had chosen to flatten herself out on the rear seat of the SUV. Her mind buffeted by the crashing of thoughts against her skull, the murder she witnessed, had evidence of, the loss of her star witness; was he nearby, was this car just returning, double checking, had she made a mistake returning. As she strained her back to look through a small gap between the pillar of the car door and one of the rear headrests, she wondered, if sometimes, she was a little too reckless. As the thought crossed her mind, a shape seemed to whip out of the car and over into the woods, the coat though, recognisable even in a glimpse. Paula knew, at that moment, as a spark flew between her belly button and coccyx, this wasn't bad luck, this was manifest prophecy.

She rearranged her skeleton carefully trying to shift weight without causing the car to rock, even with SUV suspension, she couldn't risk it. There was a second silhouette in the car, but it had seemed at rest, it could be another victim of this cult, and they could be burying bodies. Agent Staff continued her contortion between the front two seats, and over the handbrake, to grab the phone, and OTES issue self protection tazer. She placed the phone on record, and slipped it into her breast pocket, allowing the phone to rest on her homemade silicone buffer block, so she knew she could get the perfect held shot, like a real body camera, which her department were yet to receive.

Oblivious to the anxiety turmoil, turning a furrough inside the mind of Agent Staff; inside Peril's torpid leather-seated sedan, Arachni was at the base of a severe stamina drop, a trough of emotion, action, and information; leading them flickering their lids into a fretted snooze.

Arachni had been standing under the softly chattering trees for an hour, or a minute, or they were not too sure, the sky though, twisting a copera dance battle between daytime and night time, was not a usual sky. As Arachni's head swept left, the expected tree line and forest were already disintegrating, as they focused into the more acquainted contours of the banqueting hall from the lodge. Just as the sky though, the wood, so fanatically addourning and fashioning the fixtures and furnitures of the room, was more orange, or it might have been red tinged, the sound of dull footsteps on the wood, a figure that could not be seen. Or at least not yet. "Arachni?" a familiar Peril toned voice drifted in with the vision of the man himself, but again, orange tinged, like a white shirt after a mismanaged bolognaise. Not orange, red, "Arachni, it's been too long," the outstretched arms of Detective Peril like the encroaching bite from a B movie zombie. "Stop," Arachni found herself shouting. Even though they knew this couldn't be real, Arachni found themself backing toward the door to the kitchen, pressing it open and into the chromed, and tiled quiet beyond. Only, there was a familiar clear wall of window, that wasn't where it should have been, as if the had been stretched on one end, beyond its thick clarity, the forest seemed, the branches appeared to be floating in arm thick as the water. A surreal pale grey bird, with eyes too large for a normal bird, butterflew its wings, swimming up into the fading sunshine. Arachni approached to lay a hand on the fragile solidarity of the glass. Its texture, not cold, but on touching, the fingers and palms of Arachnis hands began to sink into the cooling glass, leaving them to tumble, again into the darkness of the Ocean beyond the window.

After what seemed like too long, “You are a fish,” the Ocean’s comforting surf tone interjected abruptly, “No,” Arachni corrected, trying desperately to find up, but realising quickly there was no up to find, accepting to feel thoroughly disembodied in this floating. Where are the trees? “I am not a fish, I am a human.” Arachni gave in to the curiosity to speak, to what could well be only another part of themself, their mind, talking to themself, about everything that wasn’t themselves, in a way neither party seemed complicit in conjugating . “No, there are many fish, fish only know the water, only flick their tails and make their waves close by.”. “Well what about shoals of fish then?” Arachni queried, “If a large group of fish, all made their tails flick as you say, at the same time, in a concerted effort, couldn’t they do more?.”. “Oh yes, many fish are strong, but they only know the ocean. Even big fish, lots of them, they don’t want to work together enough and make waves together.” Ocean continued nonsensically, “You be a whale, know the air, see land, make a big wave.”. “I don’t understand what you are talking about, how can I be a fish, and a whale?” Arachni, somewhat fed up with the Ocean’s inscrutable nonsense, asked with fire. “It is simple, make your brain, the biggest fish in the ocean, we all share, by not being a fish.” the Ocean chuckled to itself. “The thing about whales though Arachni,” it continued to giggle “they need to breathe….”. Arachni gasped awake, almost inhaling her own tongue in the process, sweating slightly, the leathered chair sticking to exposed skin, in the layby, under the trees.

Four seconds in, Agent Staff’s mind keeping count as she expanded her thorax, four seconds out, she repeated the process in reverse allowing the weight of her ribcage and collar bone, coupled with the squatted position, four seconds in, to allow the air to be pushed back out again for four seconds. It’s unlikely a murderer would drive around with a body propped up on a passenger seat, but the tinting effect of spying through two car windows made it difficult to find details of life. Paula continued her breathing, keeping the sound as low as possible as she crept round a depression in the muddied embankment, separating the woodland from the rest area. It wasn’t as if anyone would, or even could hear the breathing, just Paula’s own self consciousness of the act. Placing her hand to the surprisingly dry ground for support and balance, after travelling a what felt like halfway around the perimeter embankment, she peeked over the top, checking her bearing with the new car, the passenger still with a head cocked back, seemed to be casting a short condensation on the window, which was heartening. A slow creeping relief began to spread in Paula's mind, she straightened up her walk slightly, moving with less stealth, more caution, around the mudded mound; hopefully she could catch whomever it was driving on their return from the undergrowth.

Agent Staff continued her advance, slightly on the blades of her sensible hiking shoes, until, after a few premature peeps over the bluff, she could see herself in parallel with the car. Crouching slightly lower onto her knee for support, she reaffirmed the positions of the phone and the taser, pulled in her belly button to the base of her spine, coiled to strike. As she raised up, as a righteous valkyrie into battle, pushing hard off her right foot, in a purposeful blitz, up and over the raised embankment, her left foot caught in a root, she mistook for an attempt at a leg grab, causing a half turn, and self powerbomb, off the mud, on to the less forgiving loose gravel, and stone space edgings. As her chin was whipped, from her chest to the sky, on the impact of her shoulders with the floor, a long coat, and green mirrored sunglasses, began to crest over the view that was blurring out.

Some miles away from the powerbomb in the parking lot, Chip had managed to charm, or perhaps erode with sycophancy, Candi into joining him. "I just…" the sound of one large, and one normal sized engine cars, could be heard rumbling to life and then out of earshot in the distance, ".... maybe we should see what's going on." Candi concluded, hoping the danger was over, but knowing for some reason, they couldn't have entered the building before then anyway. It was that tickling in the marrow of her bones, a discomfort in remaining stationary, she got when something was about to happen. It had only happened a few times before joining the Guidance, but since then, she knew it was not to be ignored, but unsure why. Through the undergrowth the pair walked in a pseudo military recon filing, to the wooden gate. Two heavy executive sedan door clunks could be heard through the wooden slats as Candi held the handle of the gate; gently releasing the latch with her thumb and sliding in and around the door to the reflection garden, being careful to stay wide of the security light's detection. Planning tristes for some of the more married members had provided the opportunity to gain such a discrete entrance route. Maintaining a low posture, she turned, tilted her head under her raising armpit, and whispered back through the gap, "Follow my footsteps exactly, we don't want to draw attention to ourselves.". She motioned, as a lead might to a unit, with two fingers, around the edges of the hedges, to the corner of the stairs."It seems we might be alone, but trust me, we still need to be careful." Candi warned him as they drew to a stop at the stone edge of a water feature. Peering through the cool air coming off the water slowly rippling from the gently trickling water of the figure above, "I think we should move in through the lower conservatory, the door has been on the latch since last month……" Candi realised the company she was in, "Don't report me for telling you that. It's for the kitchen, there's always smokers in the kitchen."

"You just, shared your status with someone else. I thought that was forbidden?" Candi wanted to get a better understanding of Chip before entering, if he broke those rules, could he be counted on. "Oh, come on Candi, almost noone follows that rule, people can't help but compare themselves. I mean, I have quite a status, but I have always been jealous of your type.". "My type?" Candi replied with an amount of scepticism poorly hidden, "Were you not paying attention? Didn't you read the literature? Pencils, particularly with erasers Candi, are symbols of noble destiny. You don't get chronicling privileges such as myself, where I provide the ornate fill, but instead you. You're. There are those. Who are meant to guide through change.

Who's destiny is partially crystalized, like an icebreaker boat's bough, in more ways than just the ice crystals themselves, you are capable of carving new paths through what felt like a solid immovable. Of course, not invulnerable, potential land mass beneath the ice, or even stubborn ice, an eraser to the lines. Nonetheless though. Candi. You should have pride, can you not feel, our presence, here, together, is one of great importance?". The bombastic deluge had elicited a reaction of quietened, confused frustration from Candi, who had now stopped her stooping path along the lower planters of the conservatory, and was staring with one finger to her lips, the other hand holding an imaginary sandwich plate to the ceiling.

"Why talk with no mouth?" Ooda's scornfully pitched question to the still panting Rai was met with an outstretched palm of oozing purple berries, which Rai promptly wiped with disgust into the grass. "Berry bring voice, then run, but Rai not run OOda. Rai stop. Rai stop." He repeated the phrase as he continued to heave breath back into his lungs. Ooda, scooped a small amount of the berries from the ground, placing some in a leaf into her bag, with the remaining residue on her fingers, she sniffed gingerly, hoping some smell might indicate something about the mystery berry."I wouldn't eat that if you're anything like this one," a haughty voice inside Ooda's mind, she spun around, slowly 720'd, wiping the remaining residue back onto the now twice stained with purple grass. "Smart decision," the same voice, goading another twist around from Ooda, "Who?", she said to the sky, the trees, the bush she had come through. "I apologise for your friend there, it seems I might have met the wrong one. My mistake. I am Earth ambassador, Eck.".Ooda reached down for Rai, urging him to come with her, off over to where they came, away from the mouthless voices. "Oh I have a mouth, well of sorts" came the voice without a body again, Ooda hurried her pace toward the tree line. "Ooda?".

Her name, how did the voice know her name? She stopped and pushed Rai forwards through the bush in front of him, turning back and dropping low, she reasoned it must be very loud or very small to be that loud so close. "Yes,very good." the voice of Eck came through like a sarcastic conscience. "Come now, I wouldn't be here if you weren't ready to get this, I mean…. look at your friend. If you decide to follow him back that is. Too much, some of the other local, non guide types. He was open to all kinds of, not everyone is going to be nice about it you see. I am tasked to be a guide for your species to understand more about the universe. You are, apparently, the first of yours to be curious enough. But yourself, you seem ready?" These words, that Ooda had never heard before, but instantly felt an understanding for, the first real conversation she…. her mind felt as though it was crackling like embers of dry firewood. "Where?" Ooda laid flat to the grass, feeling somehow heartened by this friendly voice, which seemed to meet her own feelings of haughtiness over others.

"Just a little beyond where your eyes are moving now." the unsettling thought that it could see through her eyes, instantly answered, "Only when it makes sense to. You see we or at least I, am, to myself, a student of your species, and its time. There is a lot that we don't really need to get into. It's important to note, we do not want to interfere." Ooda did not get a new word, for the first time in her life."Or, hmm, not yet. To stop you being your sunny human selves or your own destiny. We just show the ones who need to, or find their way here, or, well there are a few ways, but we don't need to get into that now. Do you have anything to offer for your membership to the network, a memory or a song or something." Ooda reached into her bag and pulled a medium sized grapefruit she had picked as a treat the following morning from the small net hanging on her side. She broke the top quartile off, pressing her thumb in to make a bowl of juice and set it beside the now apparent small spider moving through the blades of grass toward her.

Sleep was rarely afraid, but there was something about this willowy woman's softness that set the alarms in the hallways of his mind, filled with his years of work accessing liars, on full klaxon. “Well Agent Sleep, do you mind if I call you Tom?” “Well, it seems permissions aren’t something you go for, so why even ask?” he wanted a reaction from these two, mostly her though, Sleep needed to understand what this was about, he couldn’t wait for a rescue on this. OTES as an organisation, was really an organisation that, well at his level, he might not be noticed for a day, or a fortnight, and he was not going to wait around for it, like an idiot, and if these two were it, or had a key, or a phone. “Let’s not be rude to each other, you are a guest.” her voice again too pleasant for his liking,”Guests are invited,” he cut across defiantly. “Well maybe some people in this life we just aren’t meant to get along with, but in the end it benefits us both, if you go along here. I am sure my colleague explained to you, we don’t want anything from you, we just. Your partner, is just particularly good at evading us, and we actually want to speak to her as much as she seems to want to speak to us. We just need to steer things a little, and have a few cards in our favor.”. “So I am an involuntary guest card in this weird kidnap hospital of yours? You realise that Staff has been onto you guys for ages." Tom raged definitely, "If you think it's not gonna be, they'll be coming round the mountain, or whatever, lake view this is before you will see it coming." Sleep flourished in full bluster. "Oh we will see it coming Tom, it was all seen coming, and you would know to go along, if you could see the way that we are able to." She clasped his hands in hers, the weight of the much larger bones obvious to both, maintaining his gaze, fully aware of his impotent rage. His eyes darted from his defiant stare down, and away, she knew she had won, if not his trust, then his submission to the situation. A realisation that she had the control here. "Now, you have been asked to maintain a dream journal for us during your stay, can you show us how that has been going?".

In a similarly decorated room, a few minutes prior, not too far from Agent Sleep, Detective Peril's plan was starting to come together. He had been careful to maintain as much eye contact with Lilian as he could while he had trapped the IV tube leading into his arm between two fingers. It had taken every ounce of his strength to keep it held long enough for his two former college colleagues to leave so he could, with a grimace, remove the needle entirely and make a more permanent pinch in the tube so it wouldn't be obvious it had been removed. He knew, as he felt his mind spinning, that it could be a while before his full functions and faculties would be returned.

Detective Peril was sure, as he lay, still with remnant heart palpitations and sweat accumulating between his body creases, that he wouldn't be disturbed. It had been a whole ten or maybe fifteen minutes since, what he assumed must have been an orderly, had passed to check on his status. The footsteps along what sounded to the close eyed, but awake, barely, Peril, were on a linoleum floor or some other plastic. It sounded more like a hospital, but there did not seem to be any patient noises from other rooms, if there even were other rooms. Maybe it was longer, Peril wasn't sure, but he knew, this was not the time to check an imaginary stopwatch. With great effort and purpose of thought, he clutched the crook of his elbow crease, whipped his legs across the bed, and down onto the floor under his own weight. As he brought himself up from the right angle, the effects of his stay became more apparent, his shoulders felt like they were being pulled backwards and to the floor. This was clearly going to require a lot more resistance on his part than he was used to in terms of intoxication. Maybe not even an intoxication, his mind was not fuzzy as it had been, however long ago it had been, Lilian playing with his hair, what was this drawing his knees into the floor? He felt his body weight shift back beyond his shoulders and hips, almost twerking backwards to hold himself together. The first thing here was to see if they had been foolish enough to put his belongings in the same room as him.

As he stood there, his elbow crook still feeling the tendering effects of a needle, but under the warm comfort of his palm, Peril took a moment to gain his bearings. His slightly tunnelled vision moved from corners, along walls, jerking between targets, providing very little information in the detective's addled state, other than a block-form floor map to the door, and locations of a blurred brown shape, which could be small cupboard, or another door, and bed-side table with a drawer. The drawer was Peril's first stop for investigations, it was the closest, and his mind he knew, the one he could access without a potential for misbalance. Haphazardly, he fumbled a grip, and yanked the drawer open, seeing his clothes, and surprisingly, the detective's shield, neatly stacked; emanating the soft smell of floral detergent. He tried to glance at the door for a moment to check for spectators, whipping his face without much control toward the door glass, and then back to the drawer, feeling as though his brain had bumped his skull in the process. Well, he thought to himself, if we're going to have any chance getting out of here, I need to get at least some of this on.

It took some time, skill, balance, and the special ingredient; years of drinking more than he could handle, for Peril to have such a proclivity for moving under this current sense of encumbered movement. Sliding his legs into his trousers, while perched back on the edge of the bed, he managed to catch his heel several times in each leg, as he dragged them up his thighs. He decided against buttons on the shirt, having wasted at least a minute to no avail on the fastener of his trousers, instead deciding the belt would be enough to hold them up. There were no footwear options, beside the hospital slides slid neatly just under the end of the bed. After attempting to walk in them however; Peril knew he could move neither quietly nor comfortably in them, and they were abandoned.

Peril took his first lumbered steps across the room to the tall brown box that was coming into focus. From the bed, he had assumed it was a cupboard of sorts, but as he almost fell forwards on to it, placing his hands in its middle for stability, it was confirmed. Another quick check of the reinforced glass window in the door, and Peril had opened the doors to garmentless hangers, and a piece of paper scrunched in the corner. Returning the paper to its full size, provided only one clue as to where he was; a familiar watermark on the paper.

The light of the day began to take hold, heating the air in the layby under the trees, Agent Staff's eyes flickered back into life with its intrusive brightness; her surroundings at a different angle to what she had recalled. Before the world had slipped from beneath her and delivered a power bomb that even the most experienced wrestler would struggle to shake off. She scanned the scene, she could see her own car, blocked slightly by two figures, one she recognised as the, could-have-been-corpse, but actually was a sleeping passenger riding shotgun. The car she had been approaching was now, as she peered over her shoulder, the backrest for her recovery, and two heel marks led through the gravel from her tumble to her current slump.

As she sat there on the uncomfortable floor, shifting her hips for a less jagged position, but finding none, the mirrored green glasses she recalled prior to her cut-to-black was tilting her head, the OTES issue taser hanging from her left hand. She was leaning in and whispering to the second figure, a beige leather jacketed individual, was this another member of the guidance Staff found herself wondering? It was not possible, the mirrored glasses woman was known to OTES, or at least to Agent Staff, as, if not an enemy of the Guidance, certainly a persona non grata. Guidance sources had issued security warnings not to approach her. So why were they with a member? Was it just a coincidence they were wearing beige, or a disguise? Agent Staff knew that if these two were really out to hurt her, they would have left her in the layby, maybe alive, maybe not, but this, this was concern being displayed. They might still kidnap her, or worse, she wasn't sure, but if she played this right, she knew, somehow deep in her gut, she could feel she wasn't in the danger it might have looked like from the outside. She could turn this back on them, she could use this as an opportunity.

Prior to the Agent's awakening, John had made sure to check her pockets, collecting up the taser from the unconscious pile of crumpled person, and taking a brief perusal of her pockets. The wallet contained very little in money, which John did not need anyway, but sometimes it helped to keep a stash, just in case. The wallet did yield a more important piece of information though, the laminated, officially stamped, badge of a bureaucrat. John had always tried to remain outside of the purview of OTES, ESOT, or Earth's Suppression Outreach Team. They were mostly concerned with disclosure, and John had never had an opinion or thought on it, she just followed her instinct. She had never really dealt with anything quite this wholesome before truth be told, and finding it all just a little bit tiresome to not get to use the full extent of her destined skills. Also, that chick from the woods was hot. She looked up from her searching, as a bleary eyed Arachni emerged from the car, raising two platefuls of what's-going-on-here to the sky. "You can't even go to the toilet without causing injury can you?" the slightly croaked voice of Arachni asked rhetorically. "Help me with her will you?" John hooked an arm under her shoulder and the pair pulled her body across to their car, propping her into a seated position.

John took the assorted belongings of the Agent, and went across to the SUV, "You keep an eye on her ok?" John said over her shoulder, "What do I do if she wakes up?" Arachni asked with trepidation, "I'm not like you John, people don't just, I don't fight people.". "You seemed to do just fine with that Guidance member in the woods, you'll be fine." John's word, sparking yet more curiosity in Arachni. "Wait, you saw what happened in the diner John, and the woods? Have you been following me a long time?
And you didn't step in, why? John do you even care?". She stopped with her hand on the door of SUV, turned, "It's not

about caring Arachni, this is going to get very old very fast if you keep asking me why I am doing what I am doing. Why did you pick those keys? Why did we turn left? Why did I have to pee? Why was she here in the first place?" John had released the door and taken a few steps back toward Arachni, her arms wading through her own questions as she did so. "I don't know, but what I know is they were the ones skulking in the woods with a taser Arachni." she pointed toward the slumped Staff with her chin resting on her chest. "They're from an agency. You asked about police" John tossed the wallet with the badge inside to Arachni and returned to the car door that was ajar, "Why don't you ask her?" John disappeared into the SUV, leaving only her feet sticking out, as she felt inside door pockets, footwells, and glove compartments for anything that might bring the rumble back, and mark the return to their journey, their story, the destiny.

"Who are you?" Arachni, the beige leather jacketed figure, from Staff's perspective, kicked off the interrogation, "and why are you following us?". "I was here first, you followed me." Agent Staff said defiantly, deciding to stay seated so as to appear more vulnerable, and maybe get these two to open up. "Yes, but you were the one skulking the woods with this weren't you?" John chimed in, spinning the taser in her hand. Agent

Staff switched her focus to the mirrored green glasses, "What would you have done in my position? I don't know if you realise this, but I am a federal…." Agent Staff was cut off by John chuckling. "Oh come on, you're not a federal agent like a cop. There are no stickers on the car giving detailed information on the world so many people are not ready to join yet. We weren't doing anything wrong, why did you need a weapon? Why sneak around?". Agent Staff felt a little flustered, authority was usually her best bet for advantage in a situation like this, but this green aviator-ed woman was not one to kowtow to it. "OK," said Arachni changing tack, "You were here first, but what brought you here? Let's not pretend we don't all know there is a Guidance lodge through those trees. Are you with them? Are you trying to stop us from getting to them? You know there is an actual police officer who has disappeared?" Agent Staff was used to the disrespect, and honestly agreed that she was no police officer, she considered herself above such a position. More of a politician, or spokesperson for the Earth, not a local enforcer, capturing criminals and the like. She had a higher cause, the safety of the species, the protection of knowledge. She fixed her eyes on the beige jacketed Arachni, wishing she still had her own aviators on to disguise her expression.

Eck had not ventured far on Earth, in spite of his obsession with human culture, his experiences with the current form of the species had been less than what he expected. That being said, he had never eaten something quite as good on Earth as the fruit he now sat in, enjoying its sharp but nourishing juice. "I think this will do nicely," he paused in his replenishment, "Ooda, would you like to follow me?". She had been sat cross legged on the floor, admiring the tiny spider, wondering how many other animals might also be able to talk like this. Had she hunted other animals like this? Were their howls and shrieks words, warnings, cries for help? The spider suddenly appeared on Ooda's shoulder causing her to fall backwards with shock, "Don't worry Ooda, you know that feeling you have had, as long as you can remember? The one you get trying to explain the world to the others, and the others, even Rai there, look at you, like you should be sent off to the quiet shelter. That dwelling off in the forest, where they put your mother.". Ooda felt the weight of that pain swell inside her, she had always struggled to explain to people what just came to her without effort. Thoughts that people hadn't thought, and so couldn't yet be articulated, or when they were they were dealt with suspicion. The attribution of all of her inventions to the forest itself. "Yes," she said slowly. "Well," came Eck's response with too much cheer and not enough empathy, "That's because you, well, not just you, but you got here first. You are part of a more completed human mind. There are too many parts your species ignores, from all of your years of survival against predators and the like. Truly a planet of viciousness this one. I realise a lot of this is new, but if you come with me, I can, I can save us both time and let you access the information that is already there." Ooda was stunned, and somewhat dumbfounded by this voice, what was a planet? And what did the spider mean viscous? She had seen many tribe members die at the hands of spider bites, so it was a bit rich this one being so judgemental. As the thoughts prickled the embers of her mind more, the feeling of an expanding awareness threatening to bulge out the sides of her skull, she found herself too curious not to follow.

Detective Peril had already searched the admittedly small number of places in the locked room he was detained in for anything that could help him. The various chemicals, sedatives, and intoxicants which had been forced into his system were still at war with his desire to stay standing and balanced. He flattened his body against the wall and peeked through the steel reinforced glass in the door to get a bearing, or some kind of clue of the facility he might have been held in. As he did so, and pulled his body back to the wall, a waft of a familiar smell was drawn with him, emanating from the space beneath the door. He crouched lower, flaring his nostrils to try to confirm it for himself. It was familiar, but somehow more synthetic, like the smell of flavourings in an artificial cigarette, or some kind of room freshener. The underlying familiarity though, of the purple concoction Peril knew from his own experience of the purple goo from his initiation into the Guidance, and the sachets he had found on members in his recent investigations.

The detective's ponderings were interrupted by the slapping echo sound of footsteps growing in volume towards his door. In what might have been a flash, when sober, in this state, more of a slow blink, the detective threw the cover over the bed, and stashed himself as best his body would allow, under the clothes rail in the wooden cupboard, cracking the door slightly to give a view to the door. It felt like too long for Peril, trying to maintain his balance against the weak chipboard backing of the furniture, until the door clicked open for the off white coated orderly to enter. Luckily for Peril, they seemed all too distracted with headphones and updating a clipboard at the end of the bed with a quick signature, than checking if the occupant was still in the bed. Peril seized the opportunity with a fumbling grasp. Toppling out of the cupboard, barely maintaining his feet beneath him and crashing the orderly into the wall opposite. Peril's comparative size stood in his favour in the short lived tussle with the orderly, his skills in hand to hand combat allowing him, even with a good degree of mental fog, to secure a decent choke hold. After making sure the opponent still had a pulse, Peril grabbed a set of keys from a lanyard now bunched beside the hip of the unconscious orderly. He quickly added the coat onto his own ensemble, pressed the clutch of metal and fobs to the door, and proceeded out, hoping his lack of footwear would not draw attention.

Candi and Chip had managed to slip easily into the lower rooms of the lodge, what had begun as a stooping, foot blade walk, was now more of a casual meandering through the dwelling. The pair had stopped in the security office, beneath the main banquet hall, checking the cameras for any signs of motion, and being rewarded only with the sight of blood stains on the floor of the main banquet room, and two unconscious, possibly dead, members near the main entrance. “I don’t like this at all,” Candi’s voice was stern, as you might imagine from a military commander finding their platoon drunk instead of on watch. “You see those two there Chip?” she continued rhetorically, pointing at the unmoving masses on a screen in the top left of the bank of monitors, “They’re erasers, I heard them talking to each other about it. They’re tough guys, they wouldn’t both get folded by that woman, they couldn’t. I know their partners. We need to see if they're alright.". Chip nodded, pleased to not have to control the flow events, "I'm with you Candi, whatever you need. I'm your man, guy, person" he blushed slightly hoping she hadn't thought he meant boyfriend or partner. "Did you ever think that something like this would happen? That…" Chip was by Candi and her piercing eyes turning to him, "This is a club Chip, for arachnophiles. Yeah there are some lessons taught that are….*beyond what other clubs do* but ultimately, no. I took this as a job, the membership was never in my mind, they offered it to me with options for more flexible working. I would have been crazy to turn that down, the discounts alone can be really helpful…." she trailed off, looking back to the screens, at the blood in the hall, the bodies. "I'm not that fond of all this destiny talk, you know?" she picked up again, "I have never needed to have someone else lay my road out for me, I make my own luck, my own path.". Chip smiled, "That's exactly like a pencil though.". Candi rolled her eyes, "We need to check on those two, and find out what happened in the hall, and whose blood that is."

The security office sat directly beneath the main banqueting hall, so the pair made their way somewhat carefully up the side stairway, hoping to quickly check the cameraless kitchen before investigating the blood and bodies. Chip stacked up willingly behind Candi on their walk up the stairs, enjoying the faint waft of her cassoulette as they ascended. He had been realising with an increasing certainty in her thrall, that she and he were meant for more than just some short scene, they had legs. They were not far from the top, and even with a door between them and the room, they could hear a metallic thudding, like a wooden spoon on pans."What the hell is that?" Chip asked, knowing Candi wouldn't have the answer, but hoping her confident militaristic preparedness may assuage his nervousness. Candi held up a fist like a platoon leader, turning and again pressing a finger to her lips, giving the shut-your-mouth eyes to Chip, which he enjoyed a little too much, smiling and blushing as he obliged. Candi crept further up the stairs to the door, gently releasing the handle and peering round into the stark bright, reflective chrome of the kitchen. There was no visible signs of anyone, and yet, the thuds continued, accompanied by an unintelligible echoed mumble.Candi continued her course, beckoning for Chip to follow, they followed the sound to a chrome cupboard platter stacked on the surface above. The handles to the cupboard had been jammed with several wooden utensils, as they approached, the door appeared to be bending slightly outward from the force applied. "Who's in there?" Candi asked with a pretence of courage and gentle foot kick to the outside of the door. "Get me out of here dammit!" the voice was one Chip recognised, "Chase?" he asked, already pulling the utensils from the handle, "Chase why are you in there?". The folded body of Chase, unfurled himself, with some assistance from his rescuers, from the cupboard. A large section of his face was swollen, and more puce than the reddened frustration of the remainder of it. "Why do you think I am in there you prat?" the furious Chase, having been in the cupboard sometime without help, released his aggression on the nearest target he had. "Its John, and that one from Dale's birthday.". Chase quickly went to the fridge, only to find it empty, and inside chugged water straight from the kitchen tap. "I'm going home, tell Jessop, I quit the club, I need a raise or something. I am not dealing with this side of things! I'm the business mind Chip, I am not a fighter, I don't want violence! Do you understand Chip!?" Chase grabbed Chip's lapels, raising him slightly off the ground, water from the tap still dripping off his chin. Candi placed a hand to his chest, making stern eye contact, immediately diffusing the tension. "You can do one as well Candi, I don't need this in my life." Chase dropped Chip, and stormed out of the kitchen, his footsteps disappearing down the corridor, punctuated with a very dramatic slam of the door to the lodge.

“I wonder why he’s so cross?” Chip joked, hoping to lighten the mood, “Candi, your face.”. In the darkness, it couldn’t be seen, but under the invasive brightness of the kitchen lights, it was obvious Candi too would soon have a puce section to match Chase. Chip rounded the end of the kitchen cupboard, and pulled a bag of peas from the freezer, wrapping them in a towel from the countertop before returning, attempting to press them to Candi’s face. She took the makeshift ice pack, and motioned him away, she had always found molly coddling of this type uncomfortable. “It won’t be my first black eye.” She said half laughing, hoping to soften the tension from rejecting his care.

“I know what happened to your “real” police friend.” Arachni froze, who was this person? They felt relieved but at the same time more defensive, was this a threat, was this person holding them hostage, had John checked the whole car? “You do?” they said. “I saw him, he was in the lodge, he got taken away on a gurney. I know he’s not dead. You were at a cafe and before that a strip club with him. Did you take his car from the cafe?”. “Hold the fuck on, I’m interrogating you here.” Arachni stopped this stalker in their tracks, they watched him get taken and made no attempt to do anything? “What are you doing here? More importantly, actually, I get why, why you’re following us, or me. You’re trying to stop this murder spree too.

And, your badge” Arachni wobbled the wallet with the identification folded out just far enough toward the ridgedly poised Agent, “How does this have anything to do with the Earth as whole? Do you know about all of this, quantum spider stuff,” Klo was felt in the mind of Archni, her displeasure was palpable,”We just need to understand if you want to help us stop them murdering people, or not really. I, this has been an insanely complicated few days for me and there have been dreams, and I shouldn’t even tell you. But the thing is. I want to, because everything that has been happening for this entire time, has been driven, pushed, struck, and forced on me, and, and. I need to understand that I have someone other than this maniac” Arachni gestured to the two bites deep in a sandwich, constructed from a variety of the condiments, delicatessen treats, and accoutrements sequestered from the lodge fridge, complete with flatware, John, “ who just seems to run into people and puts them unconscious or worse, dead. Tell me, you also know that out of all of this, something, makes sense to you?”

“Is this your first time in a situation like this?” the Agent’s condescension, at least as Arachni saw it, was the final straw in a hay of a day, but not as you might imagine, dried in a barn, or swirled in swiss roll slice in a field, but wet, and blown by some great turbine. “Of course it's my v t first time for the sake of breakfast…. I just really need you to understand, that" Arachni grabbed the taser, set down by the parisian-lunching John, “I will taser you, and, I will get answers.” Arachni brandished the taser, not entirely sure how it worked, but hoping the threat was sufficient. They had their finger on what felt like the trigger at least.

"Listen, I, I had a phone” Agent Staff had soiled herself the last three times she had taken taser training, it was a personal goal of hers to control it, but the suit she was in was one of her favourites, and already muddied from the floor, she couldn’t imagine having to explain both to a dry cleaner. In the end, this person was willing to share information, and could fill in some blanks from the last few days, she also might have to wear this for some time. John raised herself from a knelt eating position, and wandered forwards; manicured sandwich occasionally pecked at, and fished the phone from Agent Staff’s pocket before handing it to Arachni. “What is this about? Unlock it?” Arachni held the phone forwards for Agent Staff to unlock, still holding the taser on her for security. “What am I looking for here?” Arachni asked, staring down at the phone screen. “Play the last video.” Agent Sleep suggest-commanded.

It took a few awkward minutes, in the warming morning layby scene for the sandwich finishing John and Arachni to comprehend the vision they had seen. The callous execution of two human beings, as, a performance? That couldn't be their destiny surely? In all of this? What was "part of the journey" about any of what they witnessed? The rubber clad members dragging out the dead. Arachni was so relieved that Peril was alive, and, definitely not a friend of PFM. Equally though, the horror, of the….. Arachni had seen tragic news stories, and the internet was horrific at times, but, the heart piercing pain, of seeing, watching a serial murderer chew through two more people, not in some demonic movie scene of destruction, but a careless click of a trigger. Kidnapping the officer who was investigating him in the first place. It definitely put a dent in Arachni's confidence that John, who was now picking her teeth from the sandwich, and even this Agent, so competent they had lost their weapon and advantage, could do anything to stop PFM.

"OK, OK…..OK……OK" Arachni was stranded in a boot loop for a leadership role they had not expected to be thrust into. This Agent had evidence,"I am Arachni, what is your name?" the only words Arachni could summon to deal with the situation. “Agent Paula Staff, OTES.” Paula wiped her hand on her already muddy trousers and offered it to Arachni.

“Oh good,” said Eck, spectating the interrogation with Klo from rear window of Peril’s car, “It seems we have picked up another recruit, although, I don’t know if you saw it Klo, but, she’s a bit behind on what’s really going on here.”. Klo sighed, already knowing what was to be said, but realising Eck was determined to continue with this slow communication style. “What are you talking about now?” she said with tangible frustration. “You really haven’t gotten the hang of this yet have you Klo. You wouldn’t exactly be doing well here if I wasn’t talking you through it, you get so wound up by human communication. You need to see, this is how the humans process things, and we need to guide them, without interfering, slowly lead them. You see, if you tell them exactly in their mind, everything we know, their little brains would melt out of their ears. Also some of them might even try to operate against it, or try to speed things up, and that creates all manner of tangles, particularly with such intricate things such as these. Instead, with their words, their communication style, we must help them to be in the right places. The funny thing being of course, if we do less, they are more likely to be in the right places. You need to learn patience, Klo.”. “I know, I just, like you say Eck, I am getting used to this....laid back speed of life." she paused again for a second, trying to practise the pacing,"How are we going to get them to look into the myths without telling them, and stop all of that. They seem more focused on some dead ones.". "Klo, do you not realise who they have just met?" Eck said with surprise. "Of course I do Eck, I am practising slow human processing.". "Oh very good Klo, very good."

Peril checked his dulled reflection in the glossy room number sign, glued onto the wall outside, smoothing over his fly away hairs and straightening the clothing so he would look hopefully like just another orderly, minus shoes. He walked with as brisk a pace as his balance would allow, down the longer of the two corridor directions stretching to the left and right outside of his room. It wasn't a conscious choice, he was in instinct mode, he was following his gut, or whatever pull seemed to drag him the right direction, or in this case maybe the wrong direction, but always to the clue. If you had asked him why, he might have said it was due to the presence of fewer doors, or the blurred sign at the end that might have been an exit or stairs to an exit. Either way, Peril was approaching the first of only three doors in this direction. He stepped wide of the door, trying to hook a glance in through the window, without being observed himself. Through the glass, was an identicate room, with no bedding, and no occupant, so the detective continued his journey. At the second door however; the same glance tactic revealed three people in the room two familiar backs, and one new one, facing the door itself. Peril gave a glance over his shoulder for other orderlies before crouching down against the wall and sliding himself up under the window before peeping through. He could hear a heavily muffled conversation between Lilian and this new person, her familiar smell had seemed to either linger in the corridor or sneak under the door. As Peril lost focus, the new person caught his eye directly. Peril froze, before giving the universally recognised wide-eyed head shake of don't say anything, which this new person seemed to understand instantly. He dropped down from the window and continued off down the corridor. Now was not the time to get caught, and clearly he was not the only person they were keeping here. Where even was here, and why was this new person not sedated like he was? Peril quickened his pace, unsure of whose side this third figure was on.

"I'm just saying," said Agent Staff, having been picked up from the gravel floor next to Peril's car, "that we are likely to attract less attention if we take my SUV than your stolen..."
"Borrowed" John interjected, "Fine, *borrowed,* police car. And besides, mine is made for more terrain types, it's much more

functional.". "OK, agreed." said Arachni. "Not agreed," said John, "I don't like to be a passenger.". "What do you mean, we're all following the same lead here John?" Agent Staff was reluctant to leave her SUV in a roadside, and besides, she was the authority in this situation. "Are we?" John, now swinging her legs on the hood of Peril's car, questioned rhetorically, "I know where Arachni and I have been going. Or where they've been following, or what I've been following." she cocked her head staring out into the woods for a moment. "You could be on a different lead to us, but it just involved the same person. Or something else.". "John has a rumble she follows." Arachni explained the enigmatic half sentences for the puzzled looking Agent Staff, drawing a side eye of derision from John. "So, wait, you don't know why you're even here. I thought the whole reason the Guidance had been chattering about John is she was trying to stop them? But you have no idea at all what you're even doing? You're following a *rumble?*" Staff's voice pitch had rose to a whine by the end of her questions. "It's more complicated than a rumble, it's like the universe moving you, but you can feel the friction as it does." John said defensively; unhappy that the ability, or skill, that had kept her, and others safe so far, was being ridiculed. "I am not disputing whether it exists, or what you feel John. I just, shouldn't we work together? If we are all looking for the same person. Trying to stop the same thing. And wouldn't it be better, to be in my comfortable SUV, than.... well, a car that doesn't belong to you?". John pushed her glasses down and stared over at the SUV for a minute, looking it up and down like a motor trader accessing a junker, or a judge in a bodybuilding contest before ask-telling, "I'm driving?"

As the length left in the corridor Peril had been stalking down shortened, there was a growing smell of the chemically sweet berry that had wafted under Peril's door earlier. With occasional head turns searching the parallel walls for flickers of shadows approaching, or inward opening doors, he reached the end of the end door, with its sign from up close: "Stairs"; a concept which shook him slightly, but he pressed the clutch of keys again against the new door handle, hearing the click of the mechanism, and giving the hall walls a final detailed perimeter check, before gaining access to it.

After agreeing it was safer to travel in Agent Staff's, not stolen, or borrowed, OTES issue vehicle, John, Staff, Arachni, Klo and Eck, were travelling to the rumble of John. A rumble which seemed to have produced a deafening effect, judging from the relentless stare she was giving to the road. Barely paying attention to Staff's wittering about directions of travel. "John, I know we've covered this, but I really think we should head back to my offices, we have evidence, this could be reported, we have a case, they could go to jail, or I mean." John looked for a full 10 seconds, exactly at Staff, full right angle, while staying completely on track on the road, a half smile in the corner of her mouth, which seemed to stop the need for anymore talking about where they were going to. "Why don't you just upload it to the internet, or put it out there if you're so concerned," said Arachni. "Don't you understand?" Staff replied, craning her head backward into the section between the front seats to address Arachni directly.Shifting her hips round in the seat, legs in a kind of half yoga pose on her lap. "My job is to protect the earth from exposing this all. I know we are partners in this now, I hope, but realistically, I need to speak to you about your future." she paused sternly, causing Arachni to fish mouth. "You don't think I noticed Zelon's in this car too Arachni. This is my job, I , I am a little shocked that you didn't think I would know about. I…." she trailed off. "It's not going to look good, or help us, if I get the internet staring straight at it all, now is it. Nice to see you again by the way Eck, at least I know it's being taken seriously. And Klo, as well, I just know how important Eck has been to my species but we, already…. this is just for Arachni's benefit, they don't seem to catch up quickly in the first instance, that's all." Eck and Klo stifled chuckles to themselves. "Ah, well you know me. I never interfere, but sometimes people need to just, a little nudge, maybe, we are ambassadors first you see, a push where you were going anyway, if you think about it."

Emerging from the long accent of the stairway, in a location he still hadn't come to know, and wondering out into yet another hospital clean doorway, came a calm casual sauntering Peril, still mildly affected by the swirling chemicals in his system. His mind a rush with the themping of his heart in his ears, or, was this sometime else now. He took a less than covert swirling glance around the new corridor space. He still wasn't so sure about the way, but, there was, there had to be something. He decided during this stumbling that, there was a sound to accompany, the noise of the chemical smell entering the detective's nostrils without the need for flared nostrils or sharp inhale. The noise was almost matching what could be his heart still he thought tp himself briefly, before allowing his lead leg to pull his body along the corridor as calmly as he could muster. In part in his mind taking steps to match the sound, in case someone was listening for footsteps. Was it even the day time here? It was the kind, that of swirling clunks and general wetness you can imagine from a beer brewery, or some other distillation process.

“Does anyone have anything to eat?” Arachni asked in the hopes that John hadn’t already consumed her walk-in pantry-selection of coat provisions, complete with a bar, and cold savouries.

www.ingramcontent.com/pod-product-compliance
Lightning Source LLC
LaVergne TN
LVHW010606160826
845677LV00013B/3268

* 9 7 9 8 8 4 7 6 0 8 3 0 5 *